S0-DTC-831

Reviews

Walter Chaw, *ForeWordreviews.com*

★★★★★ An exceptional book.

About a third of the way into Wood's fantastic Vietnam free-prose collection, he ends "Unimportant," a short piece about the bloody defense of an insignificant bridge, with the words, "I have taken a picture."

In *Goodbye Vietnam,* Wood has created a series of snapshots of the absurdity of war in much the same way that Tim O'Brien did in his magnificent war idylls *If I Die in a Combat Zone, Box Me Up and Ship Me Home* and *The Things They Carried.* Similar to O'Brien, Wood has chosen the format of a loosely metered narrative described over the course of what are essentially sixty-two short-short stories. These stories range from less than a page to about three pages in length. The book opens with a dedication "To All Those We Left Behind" and ends with thirteen pages of responses to "Lies, Misconceptions, and Half-Truths" about the Vietnam conflict. The aggregate affect of these short glimpses of madness, violence, sex, and death is a breathless mélange of one soldier's descent into the darkness of war.

Though Wood occasionally betrays a classical education in his quoting of such things as Yeats's "The Second Coming" (in "Mom Calling": "What crawls my way from Bethlehem this night?"), the power of *Goodbye Vietnam* is in the visceral quality of its imagery and its emotional, absurdist rawness. Consider "The Cost of Little Boys" and its negotiation of the price to be paid to a grieving family whose child has been run over by an American military vehicle; or "Green Smoke Morning," which begins: "It's a green smoke morning. My feet are alive and screaming. My mouth is a crematorium for two million cigarettes."

Wood's work also evokes Tom Waits's hard-bitten lyricism on *Swordfishtrombone* in that it is uncompromising in its forcefully directed simplicity. The patterns of his word choice, the strength of repetition in such found phrasings as "hated-Cong" and "his cooler-than-you .45," combine into ritual - a kind of power through rhythm that marks the best of prosody and reportage alike.

Goodbye Vietnam is just as the title suggests, an exorcism of the demons of armed warfare through the brutal remembering of them. Wood's work is incandescent in its anger and brilliant in its ability to convey the importance of simple pleasures like tobacco, a cold can of Coke, and a package of cookies mailed from home to a frontline soldier who's been humping a 200-pound pack over most of Vietnam.

In a time in America's history when there is a renewed call to patriotism, *Goodbye Vietnam* will remind readers that even foot soldiers in unpopular conflicts deserve our gratitude for what they left behind in paddies not of their choosing. Robert Wood has created a thing of beauty and vigor . . .

The Book Reader

Beautifully written. A compelling, quite splendid short study that comes as close to capturing the real Vietnam War as any Socially Unacceptable authenticity can.

Leatherneck Magazine

Like pieces of shrapnel; the words sting and they go deep.

Goodbye Vietnam

Goodbye Vietnam

by

Robert W. Wood

Omonomany
Memphis, Tennessee

PUBLISHER'S NOTE

This is a work of fiction. Names, characters, places, and events are the product of the author's imagination. Any resemblance in this work to actual persons, living or dead, or to events or locales is purely coincidental.

Copyright ©2002 Omonomany

All rights reserved. No part of this publication may be reproduced, stored in a retrieval system or transmitted in any form or by any means electronic, mechanical, photocopying, recording or otherwise, without the prior written permission of the publisher, except for a reviewer, who may quote brief passages in a review.

Published by

Omonomany

5050 Poplar Avenue, Suite 1510
Memphis, TN 38157
(901) 374-9027 • Fax (901) 374-0508

Library of Congress Control Number: 2001098906

ISBN 1-59096-000-9

123456789

Printed in the United States of America

Illustration by Robert W. Wood

I was proud to serve with the 3rd Marine Division in the Republic of Vietnam. I served with no distinction; neither proving an exceptional coward or any kind of hero. The prose poems in this work are snapshots of moments remembered. They are suspended in an uneasy tranquility, and they will always be part of me for I will never be that important again.

Now that I grow old, and recollecting is my trade, in all the recollections that I polish and rewind; still these shadows linger in the corners of my mind.

Robert W. Wood

GLOSSARY

Bangalore Torpedo--Cylindrically shaped charge designed to blow a path through perimeter defenses (concertina wire, mine fields, etc.).

Boom-Boom Girls—Prostitutes.

Buying the Farm—Dead (refers to six feet of farm land).

Buying a Stone—Dead (refers to headstone for grave).

Claymore—Mine, antipersonnel.

Comshaw—An artist in the procurement of supplies.

Grungy—Having a worn and experienced look.

Gunny—Sergeant E-7. Usually people of great knowledge and wisdom in their trade.

Hog—.50 caliber, belt-fed, heavy machine gun.

In-Country—Service in Vietnam.

John Wayne Crackers—Round, virtually bulletproof crackers in C-Rats.

Ka-Bar—Standard issue knife for Marines.

Klick—Kilometer

L—Ambush formation shaped like an L to interdict a trail, pathway or route of approach.

LBJ Trail—The route to Vietnam. Named after President Johnson.

LST—Landing Ship Tank. Vessel used for transporting troops and heavy equipment to the shore.

Number One—Vietnamese slang for "the best".

Piastras—Vietnamese currency.

Pogue—Marine slang for someone who is useless. Derived from Korean word meaning catamite.

Popular Forces—Republic of Vietnam militia units consisting of lightly armed and lightly trained villagers. Their mission was to protect their village and the surrounding farm land from the Viet-Cong.

RPG-Rocket Propelled Grenade

R&R—Rest and Relaxation.

Spider Hole—Extremely small, well camouflaged firing position used by snipers.

Thog—Armored personnel carriers used for providing transport, fire support and mechanized assault. A two tracked vehicle capable of negotiating marginal terrain and usually armed with one .50 caliber heavy machinegun, and one or two .308 caliber machineguns.

DEDICATED

TO

ALL THOSE

WE LEFT BEHIND

OPENINGS

A bus dressed in olive drab stops and a big, ugly man in green steps off. He looks mad. I don't care a great deal because there are thirty of us, and I figure it will be difficult to be mad at all of us simultaneously. I am wrong.

He states emphatically that he is Drill Sergeant Granada and he hates our frigging, pogue guts. The man has a lot of credibility. I believe him instantly. He appears to be just on the verge of attacking all of us. I have the feeling our very existence is a curse unto his soul, and that he is exercising inhuman self-control to keep from tearing us limb from limb. This is the first time I have ever truly understood the concept of original sin.

We are marched onto the bus and told to sit straight and keep our frigging mouths closed unless addressed by the Sergeant. The Sergeant walks back to the biggest recruit on the bus. The Sergeant is about five feet, seven inches tall and maybe weighs in at 120 pounds. Everything on the Sergeant shines out at the world—every button, every perfectly starched angle of his uniform, his shoes, and especially his eyes which are centered by burning lamps of madness.

The recruit's name is Stenoski, and he is so big, I can't imagine he has any more sides than the one I can see. The Sergeant bends down until his face is a quarter of an inch from Stenoski's nose. Then he screams with a voice that fills time up like a rain barrel being poured into a thimble. He fills up today, then yesterday, and the day before. His words run together as if they are afraid of what will happen to them if they don't keep moving. "What the frigging hell are you doing on my bus, you baby faced, shit eating, elephant maggot?" Stenoski appears to have been turned to stone. Then all of him winces and he looks up at the Sergeant. This is a gross error in judgement. The Sergeant screams even louder, "Don't eyeball me, maggot. You lard-assed maggot, keep your eyes straight ahead. If I want you to look at me, I'll pull them out of their sockets and put them on my sleeve. Do you understand your beloved Sergeant Instructor?" This last is delivered in a whisper of interrogation.

At the whisper, Stenoski turns his eyes to the Sergeant to say, "Yes sir." The Sergeant strikes Stenoski over the head with a little stick he is carrying tucked under his arm. He screams even louder than ever. The whole thing seems to be too much for the Sergeant to bear. All the world order has been destroyed and the dogs of chaos are loose. I realize nothing I have ever witnessed is as bad as what Stenoski has done. Somehow I know Stenoski has committed an unforgivable sin. I would gladly kill Stenoski, but I am afraid to move my eyeballs.

WHEN I GROW UP

"Don't eyeball me, shit-face." Someone hits me in the stomach. I don't know who because I can't eyeball him. To look upon his face is to see God. The Bible was right, the consequences are awesome.

"Move! Move! Move!"

The voice comes from everywhere and I am inside the burning bush. My mind is three paces behind whatever I am trying to catch. Lord, how I wish to respond with alacrity. I wish to be the essence of speed. Alas, there are dragons shitting fire in my mind, and my hands and feet are encased in mammoth rubber bands.

To be last is to be dead, worse than dead, because the dead cannot hear the Sergeant Instructor. His every word is a scream; he has a thousand eyes. His voice bursts within you like an explosion of silver fishhooks.

His voice is my grandfather in a rage, my father demented with my shortcomings, my mother appalled by such clumsiness, the giant policeman at the corner watching, God's wrath in dreams remembered and the thoughtfulness of everyone who ever beat the hell out of me. His voice is everyone I ever wished to please and couldn't. When I grow up, I want to be just like him.

THE GIFT

"I am going to take that little shit-eating grin, maggot. You got that?" Said by my beloved Sergeant Instructor as he sticks his nose on my nose. "Sergeant Instructor, the candidate fully comprehends the clever choice of words made by the Sergeant. . ." A sharp blow is delivered to my stomach by my beloved Sergeant Instructor and my breath goes somewhere I cannot find it.

I am braced against the bulkhead. I have aspirations of melting into it.
"You know there is a commission of civilian pogues meeting here today, shit-for-brains?"
"Sergeant Instructor, the candidate is fully aware of the meeting in question."
"Do you know they are meeting to determine if any of you toads have been struck or otherwise abused by your beloved Sergeant Instructor?" Said while the Sergeant Instructor grinds his boot into my boot.
"Sergeant Instructor, the candidate is appalled by the perfidious calumny being spread concerning..."

A massive blow is delivered to my solar plexus. Jesus! I love this man. There is nothing too good for this man.
"Have you ever been struck, or abused in any manner by your beloved Sergeant Instructor, you rat-faced puke?"
"Sergeant Instructor, the candidate wishes to voice his concern for the immortal soul of anyone so mendacious as to describe your treatment as abusive or..." Another blow finds its way to my solar plexus, but I am prepared and only small parts of my breath die. I see only a couple of minor constellations and escape the panorama of the whole galaxy.

"Out of my sight, you shit-faced pogue. Move! Move! Move!" Ah, with what speed I am moving. Einstein is baffled as the speed of light drops behind. I spit on such mundane limitations that do not enjoy the propulsion system of the Sergeant Instructor's wrath. Christ! I am falling. The Sergeant Instructor's boot has tripped the greater than the speed of light vehicle. I and all my paraphernalia are hurtling toward the earth. Rifle, helmet, light marching pack, web belt with two canteens, one first aid pouch, one bayonet, one scabbard, and four ammo pouches are coming with me. Sorry, fellows.

God! I just love this man. What a sense of humor, a veritable prince among men, an ambassador of goodwill, a magus bearing gifts for all, a . . . The magus has just delivered a gift to my shin. "Move! Move! Move!"

IN-COUNTRY

We are headed in-country. Marines lay scattered through the bowels of a huge C-130. There is little conversation. Each person seems lost in his own reverie of expectation.

The plane begins its descent into Da Nang. Someone yells to hold on. The last time the Marines landed was in 1845 under the command of Captain John ("Mad Jack") Percival to rescue a French bishop. We have given up rescuing French bishops, but we have always got a "Mad Jack."

None of the new-kids-on-the-block know what to expect. In the way of such things, however, none of us ask. Where are the sounds of war?

The ramp descends and we are herded off by a Sergeant. He looks very grungy in faded cammos and bronze tan. I feel awkward and embarrassed by my shiny new cammos and pallor.

There are signs for each battalion set up in a large, empty hangar. We are told to take our orders and assemble under the appropriate sign.

The C-130 that brought us is being loaded with shiny coffins. They are carried by an olive drab forklift. The coffins are stacked three across and three deep. Everyone has seen them. The old hands seem oblivious to their presence. The new kids look only once directly, then look away pretending to be concerned with other things.

We do not know the proper etiquette and are embarrassed by our ignorance. Each of us projects a lack of interest and finds other small tasks to camouflage our inadequacy.

The flash of stacked aluminium coffins propelled by a forklift seems bizarre. This is the only sign of a war in progress. There are no wrecked vehicles or tracers overhead. Everything seems normal. Everything is neat and organized. Where is the war?

THE MOVIE

"A class in forengal metacopulation will be given in the communications bunker by Major Hemhurst at 0800 hours." That is written on a C-ration box stuck on our bunker and every other bunker in the neighborhood. Everyone knows who wrote it. Even Major Hemhurst knows. It was the officer. He is always doing things like that. Everyone in the platoon has "Epaminondas Lives" stencilled in red paint on his helmet. If you ask him what it means, he just says he doesn't know, but Major Hemhurst made him put it on everybody's helmet. Once I was leaning against a thog (it was really an armored personnel carrier but he called them thogs and pretty soon everyone else did too, even Major Hemhurst) and I said, " This war sucks." I didn't mean it. I just said so because of the silence. He kicked my boot hard. "Carruthers, you ass, this is not a war, this is a movie . . . a bad movie, but a movie; and I know because Major Hemhurst told me, and he's right because sometimes I hear the camera whirring, and the camera crew talking, and the scenery rolling around, and the lights going on and off, and the guy with the sheet of tin who makes the thunder, and a lot of things you don't notice because you are an enlisted son-of-a-bitch and I know because Major Hemhurst told me." And he was right too.

WILL YOU SEND FOR ME?

At a small crossroad on Route 1 leans a shack of coca-cola cans, spider webs, C-ration cartons, and packing case wood. Here you can purchase hot coca-colas, candy bars from the black market, ponchos and all kinds of Marine Corps equipment. You can trade money here, open a bank account in Switzerland, place wagers on coming battles, buy a sweepstakes ticket or talk to the proprietor about America.

The proprietors know all about America. They have learned from twenty year old magazines and eighteen year old Marines. A dream has been fashioned.

Three people work in the shack—a Vietnamese male who limps in order to explain why he is not in the army, a female who is probably his wife, and an incredibly beautiful twelve year old child. The shack squats on a road leading to a battalion head-quarters. There is much traffic. Everyday Marines stop and tell the people in the shack about America.

People have been stopping every since the war began. The say-ings about America are piling up. They have filled the entire shack and have to be stacked outside. The Vietnamese are very neat and the sayings are stacked perfectly row on row. The Vietnamese are grateful for these sayings. They are very polite. The beautiful little girl always asks, "Will you send for me when you go America?" Almost everyone says they will send for her and she smiles very happily. On the counter where she rests her hands the words "will you send for me" are chiseled in the wood and just above lie the same words in French and Japanese.

PEOPLE NEW TO KILL

The river is a quiet brown. It is filled with laughter and dancing children. A village of tree-houses-fallen-to-the-ground sits nearby. We are washing ourselves and the thogs because there is no one left to kill in the neighborhood.

The officer has placed security around and about, but not even he believes the Hated-Cong are waiting here at 1300 on a Wednesday. We are playing in the river and communicating with people that we may win their hearts and minds. Children always seem to like us.

I think mostly they like candy and C-rations, weapons and uniforms, strange language and funny customs. These are children of the countryside, a different breed from the cityside. These are diffident with smiles waiting. The city children have hands of grab, smiles for advertising, and filthy pictures for sale.

We are at ease with the city children because they do not embarrass us with their humanity. The children of the countryside have eyes of wonder, and they are fragile and easily broken by the clumsy green giants from across the sea. After they are broken, they are put together again with hard little eyes, and the used minds of advertising executives. Only death will break them again.

These children here have not been broken yet. They flock to us. It is difficult to explain to them where they cannot flock— our rifles, the big weapons on the thogs, and all the other dangers that accompany us. They cannot understand our strange customs and language.

It is amusing to almost everyone to teach them our language.

Curse words are very popular. Some words will kill us.

The officer is entertaining himself by telling the biggest child that he is a number one punk. The biggest child repeats to the officer, "You numah one punk." The officer roars with laughter and nods his head. He tells biggest child that all American officers are number one punks. Everyone is laughing. The world is laughing, the river giggles, the ground shakes and we are living in a small town in Wyoming on a fourth of July picnic. Who knows where the war has gone?

Then biggest child goes over to the side of the thog to talk to Willy. Willy is the smallest Marine in the world and he is a prototype for every punk created between 1945 and 1950. These were bad years for punks.

Willy has been beaten up by everyone and everything he ever fought. No one ever liked Willy, except maybe the officer who loves everything that's broken.

Why in all of time should biggest child and smallest Marine come together on the banks of the Song Bien Ky on June 2, 1967? (If you know the answer to this question, I will find you and kill you.)

Biggest child, a great smile upon his face, screams at Willy, "You numah one punk." Biggest child waits for his approval. Smallest Marine grabs biggest child and hurls him into the Song Bien Ky on June 2, 1967. After biggest child he hurls a magnificent twenty foot long stream of curses. This is interrupted by the officer.

The officer is holding smallest Marine under the water. The officer is saying that Willy has killed him, that he has written his death in the waters of the Song Bien Ky on June 2, 1967.

Biggest child has emerged downstream. His hate, like sunlight on a mirror, flashes around us. "I be Cong. I go Cong." Biggest child disappears into the village.

The officer has stopped drowning Willy and is staring into the village where biggest child disappeared. The officer is very sad. We are all very sad, even Willy. The river is quiet brown, emptied of laughter and children, and there is someone new to kill in the neighborhood.

BODIES TO COUNT

Body count is all the rage these days. At the local level, we seldom indulge in such boorish pursuits except in moments of passion. However, it is necessary to placate Battalion from time to time. This is one of those times.

Everybody knows that one Marine is worth ten gooks. No, wait, I think that's Ivans and Chinks. Gooks, we are worth maybe twenty. Consequent to this, Battalion expects the body count to reflect these realities.

Statistics are catching on at every governmental level. We are heavy into counting. We count all the ammunition we expend and all we have left. We count our dead. We count our wounded and, most of all, we count the days left in-country.

The officer has developed an efficient body count system. It is all based on reason and reality. A dead body is a dead body and what is the best place for collecting these little rascals? A cemetery.

After every fire-fight we go dig up a few and cart them off to Battalion to be counted. Some of these bodies are not in the best of condition. "Lieutenant, these damn things are decomposed. They must have been dead ten years." "Yes sir, we are the meanest damn Marines in the world. We not only kill the sons-of-bitches, we decompose them on the spot."

It does get tiresome digging up new ones, so the officer got a better idea. We took thirty of our best bodies and had them bronzed. "Lieutenant, what are these damn things? They look like they've been bronzed." "Yes sir, we are the meanest damn Marines in the world. We not only kill the sons-of-bitches, we bronze them on the spot."

MOM CALLING

The muzzle flash lights up my night and frames in grimace the face of a Hated-Cong. Welcome to hell, my friend of the night.

Head arched, skull and brains like tiny phosphorescent stars spray across the night. Darkness comes again and after images descend upon my eyes. How many more? What crawls my way from Bethlehem this night?

I am a child lost on a dark street far from home. I cannot imagine ever wanting to be beyond my parents' reach. Why are they not with me?

I am wet with another's death. I am comforted, but I am desperately alone. Don't leave me here, mom. Mom! Mom! I'll be home for dinner right on time. I'll brush my teeth, I'll eat my lousy carrots, and I'll make good grades in school forever. Mom!

Sh! Sh! I can hear them. The Hated-Cong are asking for their mothers in their little gibberish tongue. I have to kill the bastards so mom can hear me call.

BACK-COUNTRY

I am in back-country. Pogue land. A platoon of thogs has been sent for two days of refitting and maintenance. The location is about half a klick northwest of Da Nang. There is ice, cold cokes, ice cream, warm showers, three hot meals a day and movies four nights a week. This is utter madness and even my large white rabbit is bewildered.

Here the war is out of focus, an afterimage hanging on the periphery of vision. People salute here and wear clean, dry clothes. The officers and NCO's keep their pistols in pistol bags so they won't get dirty. All weapons must be kept unloaded except during guard duty. Only the Marines on the perimeter carry weapons.

There are bunkers and slit trenches, but the Marines sleep in large tents with wooden floors, spring beds and mattresses made by local Vietnamese entrepreneurs. There is plenty of cold water, Kool-Aid, and Coca-Colas. These are all miraculous gifts to troops that have been in Indian country for three months and will soon return.

I will never have enough water again as long as I live. You cannot appreciate the utter, maddening joy of being water rich until you have experienced the parched despair of the water poor. Your mouth feels like charred and blistered paint on a steel floor. Every thought, even unto death, is of cold water cascading down your throat.

The first cold Coke is not within the reach of dreams. Each Marine holds the glistening can for a moment embracing the miracle of ice-cold beads of water running down it's sides.

The can is emptied gently in small gulps of stinging-sweet liquid heaven.

The hot meals are eaten in virtual silence as if concentration was needed to insure the dream did not fade. The back-county Marines are laughing and talking in a world of take-for-granteds. The boondock Marines are quiet and solemn, as if they had been dropped into a monastery full of holy relics from their past.

At night all the boondock Marines go to the movie. It is shown outside on a plywood board covered with a sheet. The picture is about a lot of bikini clad girls on a beach. During the film tracer fire can be seen in the distance and a nearby battery of 105's begin firing on-call rounds.

Tomorrow we will head back to the boondocks. About a klick down the road we will pass a sign that says, "You are leaving Pogue country." A new movie will begin.

THE LOGIC OF WAR

We have stopped half a klick from the ville. It has always been a friendly place. They have never even had a Popular Forces outfit. The ville is close enough to Battalion that there has been no need.

Today something is wrong. There is no one in the fields. No noise. No laughter of children. No movement can be seen.

The officer sends thogs out to flank the ville at a safe distance, out of RPG range, but still well within the range of our .50s. Then he orders a recon squad to the ville. He has his map out and we know he is getting ready to call in artillery support if the shit hits the fan.

The twelve man squad and a sergeant move toward the ville in four man fire teams. They come in from the flank to allow the main body to have direct fields of fire. The four man teams displace forward one at a time with two teams forming a base of fire for the team in motion. The fire teams alternate, but not in any set rotation that the enemy could predict. There is still no activity in the ville.

Each thog has been assigned a cone of fire to cover the entire area. We have even put out a fan of rearguard security. There is no treeline for two klicks, just nice open paddies. The ville is the only place to hide.

The first team has entered the ville. There is a wave of expectation that washes over us. We know what the team is feeling. Most of us are glad we are back here.

The officer is on the radio talking to the squad leader who is now in the ville. We move in a crescent formation toward the ville, leaving the east side to be covered by fire from the flanks. Hopefully this will protect us from the outrage of "friendly fire." Where do they get these terms?

As we sweep in force through the ville one Marine on each flank stands in clear view of the support elements to mark the progress of friendly forces. If we get hit they will mark their positions with smoke grenades.

There are no Cong in the village. They have come and gone. Six heads are stuck on poles at the east side of the ville. Suddenly all the people in the village are screaming and wailing. They have waited for the sweep to be completed fearing the Cong had set a trap.

The village administrator and five elders are heads on poles. Their wives and children are pulling their hair and beating their breasts as they mourn the dead. There are pools of blood. Six discarded bodies lie in a pile. It is impossible to accept the reality that thrashes around us.

The interpreter, Sergeant Thieu, says the Cong came in around 0200 hours. There were six of them. They gathered the villagers together and lectured them on the evil and stupidity of supporting the puppet government in Saigon. They bound the six men and slit their throats. They told the villagers that only the Cong could protect them. A rice tax was set. Four young male villagers were given the opportunity to join the Hated-Cong. No one refused the offer. They left at 0300 hours, just one hour. Just one hour.

We can see it in their faces. They know we cannot protect them from this horror. They know we too are to blame for we have not lived up to our promises. They wish to be free to raise their crops and live out their time with their families. They have fought for this freedom longer than America has existed, against the Han Chinese, the Chams, the Mongols, the Dutch, the British, the French and the Japanese.

They see time differently. They are here til the end, or their end. They understand the logic of what the Cong have done. They now know that we do not comprehend their war. They know.

On the east side of the ville the tracks of the Hated-Cong are clear. They walked through the sucking mud of the rice paddies straight toward the nearest treeline. The Indian reports six men came in walking on the rice paddy dikes and ten men left walking directly across the paddies. A very nice trail indeed. Here chickey, chickey.

Battalion is notified. Soon South Vietnamese troops will arrive. Some kind of defensive unit will be established. Villagers will be relocated. More troops will be tied down. Six men have accomplished the work of a battalion.

We form an inverted V formation with two thogs in the lead. About half a klick from the treeline the formation halts. The officer gets out of the lead thog and fires a full magazine into a paddy dike. The new-boys-on-the-block think he has gone round the bend. The old hands know he is about to call in artillery to blow hell out of the treeline.

Our latest piece of madness is a directive that we are not to call in artillery unless we are under fire and getting our ass kicked. Now we are under fire and the officer will kick anybody's ass that says otherwise.

The first artillery round is a white phosphorous marker round that lands about 200 meters into the treeline and about 150 meters north of where the tracks of the Hated-Cong enter the treeline. The officer adjusts, then fires for effect. Massive clouds of dirt and debris are blown skyward. The officer walks the barrage across an area 600 meters deep and 400 meters wide. The Cong should have been waiting for us about 200 meters in, just enough to get all of us in the killing zone of their ambush. The point of the V moves into the area devastated by the barrage. All our major firepower remains outside the treeline, able to maneuver and flank anything that is left.

The artillery rounds have variable time fuses on them to set the rounds off about twenty feet above the ground. When they explode, massive amounts of shrapnel are hurled in all directions toward the earth. The trees also make excellent shrapnel.

We find eight bodies, one heavy machinegun, four AK-47s and six RPGs. One of the bodies is a twelve year old villager with his hands tied behind his back and another rope tied to his throat. None of us know his name, but we know he has become a casualty of the logic of war.

TODAY'S SPECTATORS

We are sitting on Hill 55. A grandstand has been set up and there are peanuts, popcorn, and hotdogs. About a klick away, the Hated-Cong have put out some old Samsonite folding chairs. Rice balls and fish are available. It is a very clear day. The announcer is mouthing the usual cliches about perfect weather conditions for a sporting event.

In front of us stretches Route 1 leading into Da Nang. On the road there is a column of South Vietnamese trucks, tanks and personnel carriers. The column is almost a klick long.

The announcer tells us there is an argument between two rival government factions. The fans are told to stay off the playing field and just watch the game. Like we were going to volunteer to participate.

Above the column are four Skyraiders. These planes are dearly loved by Marines. They fly low and slow and are heavily armor plated for taking ground fire. They carry an amazing amount of ordinance and can actually hit the targets you give them. The Cong hate the little devils.

It's four Skyraiders against a klick of trucks, tanks and personnel carriers. The opposing captains have been fitted with mikes so the spectators can get the feel of the action. The Skyraiders have won the toss and elect to come in out of the sun.

One Skyraider peels off from the circle and passes over the column at about 1500 meters. The Skyraider captain tells the convoy commander to halt the column and return to the sideline. The column halts. The planes continue to circle. Then the column starts again.

Another Skyraider swoops down. This one passes over the convoy at 1000 meters with guns blazing. Thousands of tracers pour from the column with no visible effect. Vehicles are hit all along the column, but it continues to move.

Another Skyraider peels off. This one banks a hard left and heads for the deck. He disappears behind a small knoll beside Route 1. Suddenly he reappears heading flat out down the center of the highway about fifty feet above the pavement. His propeller is kicking up dust. Three hundred meters from the front of the convoy he opens up. Vehicles are shredded like confetti.

Jesus! Who is this guy? Sign him up now. Get that dude quick. We are talking Pro Bowl here. The Marines are cheering like mad. The South Vietnamese infantry are pouring out of the vehicles for the relative safety of nearby ditches. The captains are transmitting again. The convoy commander has had enough. The column will turn back, but the captain demands a number one draft pick. This is a movie. I knew it, I knew it all along.

THINGS WHICH WILL DIE
AND MAKE YOU SAD

There are many dogs in this country. These dogs are poorly cared for because the cruelty to animal people, the dog pound, veterinarians, and dog care specialists are conspicuously absent. The dogs know this and they are very sad. Each year they vote a straight Democratic ticket and still nothing comes of it. This is not a good country for dogs. Each year more dogs leave the country to go to the big city where they hope things will be better.

The Americans have made a big difference for the dogs. It is the belief of most canines that Americans will be their salvation. They constantly hang around our bases trying to make a case for better treatment, self government, a balance of trade, more economic support and birth control. The dogs are always in the way trying to communicate their feelings. Americans give them handouts and pet them and play with them and say soothing things. They do not listen to what the dogs really want because they are too busy giving handouts.

Today all the Americans are hiding in their bunkers because this is Vietnamese National Kill-All-The-Dogs-On-American-Facilities Day. An American soldier was bitten by a dog and had to get medical attention. The dog was trying to tell the soldier about self-government, when the GI attempted to force feed him some M&Ms.

The Vietnamese decided it would please the Americans if they killed all the dogs. The pleasing of Americans is a lifestyle here. Today we are hiding in our bunkers while the Vietnamese kill the dogs. We do not wish to see this because we are extremely nice people.

THE COST OF LITTLE BOYS

Out across the desert we are running. In the thogs are ammunition and supplies for Company C waiting in a far away oasis.

I sit behind the great gun watching the world pass. The swift motion with the wind in your face and the spray of sand behind us is good. The world is flat and open - safe.

The great gun can reach far and only fools would disturb our journey. Here on the desert there are few places for fools to hide.

We are coming to one of these places. The possibilities are small, however. It is a tiny oasis with a group of Vietnamese who are relatives of the people living in the nearby leper colony. Even the Hated-Cong fear them.

All the guns turn toward the oasis as we pass. Suddenly there is motion from behind a small sand dune directly in front of us, then a thud under the lead machine.

The thogs fan out and Marines scatter from their bowels across the dunes. Only the wind speaks and the blood pounds. Will they kill us with anxiety, mother dear?

Then the officer is screaming for a medic. There is something caught in the tracks of the lead thog. We have caught a small child.

The medic is useless. There are patches of child, red and pink, woven into the tracks of the thog. An old woman screaming comes from the oasis.

Little Bobby has been struck by a car. The police and the ambulance will be here soon. There is organization and insurance and courts of law to decide the issue.

Bobby's mother is made from massive webs of wrinkles. If you caught the thread just behind her ear and pulled she would unravel somewhere beyond Christmas. She is wailing and pulling her hair. Her speech is faster than the ear can follow.

We do not know what to do. We are embarrassed and many look down and shuffle their feet. Our interpreter, Staff Sergeant Ky, is not embarrassed. He is very wise.

The officer and our wise man are talking to the ancient one. Then like small, gray shadows, the rest of the village is perched upon the dune. They too are wailing and the wind has begun to cry.

The wise man and the ancient one are locked in speech. First one raises his voice and the other is head shaking, then the other raises her voice and relinquishes the head shaking. This goes on for four days and four nights and the sun does not shine. Then both the wise man and the ancient one nod their heads wisely. The spectator shadows nod their heads wisely.

Staff Sergeant Ky gives the ancient one 500 piastras, and beside the massive tracks of the thog, Bobby nods his head wisely. We are running across the desert and the wind feels just as good as always.

BECAUSE OF DANNY-
WHO-SCARED-ME-TO-DEATH

I am in a hooch with a stone basin for feeding pigs, or sacrific-
ing virgins, or hiding behind. Shit! I am prone-crawling. Many
people are trying to kill me. Tiny noise holes are being made in
the air. Bursts of color blossom. Rampant flowers of death
spring from the earth nearby. I must keep telling myself I am
no hero.

Sometimes as a child in the dentist's waiting room, I had the
same feelings. I am going down the hall toward the chair. I am
creeping into the chair. I do not look at anything now. I look
only beyond this time. It will pass.

But Danny-Who-Scared-Me-To-Death has never passed. He
lives in my mind. He is bigger than most things from childhood remembered. I was 14 years old when Danny appeared in
a tiny corner of my life and swelled up to knock hell out of an
entire day.

Danny was a year older than me and maybe six feet taller. I was
the boss of my block—it was a very small block with very small
kids. We were playing ball in the street when Danny and a
group of his friends rode up on their bikes. Two thirteen year
old sporting ladies were watching.

We milled about for a while like two packs of dogs sniffing each
other. Then I said something perfectly hilarious to Danny. The
next thing I knew I was on my face in the gravel in the street in
another part of time and Danny was saying "Do you give?"
Someone inside of me said "Yes" before I could stop him. Danny
got up and stood off watching me rise. I didn't say anything.

No one said anything. Then one of the sporting ladies started giggling. (I still hear that giggle sometimes.) Everyone seemed embarrassed, even Danny. Later everyone went to Herman's Drug Store and had cherry cokes. Danny bought mine and talked to me a lot because he was about half happy and about half embarrassed. I never drink cherry cokes anymore.

Danny-Who-Scared-Me-To-Death is out there now and I can hear the giggles. I am up moving toward the hooches and trench system on the north side of the village. Billy and Joey and Liz and the old crowd are watching. I'm killing everything. I can't seem to miss. They are just as surprised as I am. This is not supposed to happen—just stand up, start walking casually, shoot, and smile into insanity. They do not know that I already died of Danny-who-scared-me-to-death. I am in the trench. The squad is coming.

I have put many holes in Danny—face in the dirt, past caring, no giggles heard. My turn. Now quiet comes, old handshakes, slaps on the back, cigarettes and canteens. Soon we are about half happy and about half embarrassed. We all go down to Herman's Drug Store for cherry cokes, but none of the Dannys can come.

UNIMPORTANT

There is a bridge near Phong Dien constructed by elves. This bridge was made from babies' breath, buffalo manure, and IT&T stock certificates.

The span of this bridge has been cantilevered randomly by a poorly placed explosive charge. It is a very unimportant bridge and, consequently, rated a very unimportant explosive charge, placed by a very unimportant Hated-Cong. The bridge knows all of this and looks very forlorn believing itself destined never to appear on American news programs.

An unimportant company of Marines guard the workers reconstructing the bridge. A company of Vietnamese Popular Forces have dug in around the southern approach to the bridge for no apparent reason. The officer offered them four apparent reasons, but they refused to accept any of them.

The PFs are rainbows of color—basic black pajamas, red and yellow kerchiefs, camouflage cowboy hats, pink garterbelts, and white bucks. During the day they harass traffic on the highway, asking for everyone's IDs and waving their antiquated weapons in parabolas of terror ignored. They smoke cigarettes until their teeth melt, chatter constantly, poke fingers in every orifice, and gaily flaunt a total absence of organization. The officer claims they are a crack military outfit cleverly disguised to lure the Hated-Cong into our midst.

The PFs love us. They love attempting to sell us all sorts of unwanted bric-a-brac: kerchiefs, air mattresses, soy sauce, dead fish, and misunderstandings. They like, and want, everything American: Coca-Cola, cigarettes, canned food, butane lighters, and misunderstandings. They giggle, they prance, they put their paws on your shirt and, come every election, they vote a straight Republican ticket. God, they want to please.

The officer will not allow the PFs to enter our perimeter. He says they may catch galloping amadosat—a maddening desire to make sense out of everything. We are also told to notify the officer if we see the PFs pulling out.

For twenty-two days they cavort around seemingly without a care. On the twenty-third day they leave quickly, quietly with little bird flutters. They do not wave bye-bye.

The officer puts us on 100% alert. The wire is rechecked, claymores are inspected, weapons are cleaned, and fields of fire re-emphasized. We practice being surrounded, have a square dance, kiss the world good-bye, and wait.

They come quietly into our dark night at 0300. They run toward the wire—dark colors, empty-solid in the night, turning, twisting, screaming ever onward. Sounds beat on us like great, soft hammers. Their mortars come, our mortars come, our eight inchers come.

In the morning we watch the slivers of first light touch gently on the bits and pieces of people-in-the-wire. Three of us are dead and eight of us are wounded. Their are eighteen people-in-the-wire and two of them are dressed in rainbows, pink garterbelts and white bucks. The bridge is here, unimportant still, but I have taken a picture.

NO ONE DIES

Every once in a while, and once upon a time, the officer says "No one dies." When the darkness comes lonely and the wind cries, you begin to believe him even though the sunshine believes otherwise.

Two days ago, near Hill 22, Rogers and Stubby bought the farm. They were speckled by automatic weapons fire while in the performance of their duty.

Today the officer had to go to Charlie Med to identify the bodies. An officer has to look at everyone who buys it and sign a form that states he recognizes the dead man.

I don't normally drive for the officer, but today he asked me to drive him. When I asked him why, he said, "Because you work on a farm and should know a vegetable when you see one."

At Charlie Med we went into this big, cold room that lasted two days and the doctor pulled out two body trays. Rogers and Stubby were lying on the trays. The officer didn't look at either one of them. The doctor handed a paper to the officer and asked him to sign as having identified the bodies.

The officer turned to him saying, "You simpleminded knave, you afterthought of a harlot, you spawn of a minor equation. An excessive amount of adipose tissue and a deficiency in gray matter is no excuse for the attempted perpetration of such a heinous hoax upon the troopers of the People's Marine Corps. Only my belief that ignorance, rather than intelligent design, prompted this all too lavish display of bad taste prevents me from turning you over to one of the People's Commissars for immediate solution."

The doctor, after going through a few stages of color variation, had begun to revive. "You can't talk to me like that. I'm a Major . . . I'm a doctor."

"Indeed! You are unequivocally enough of an ass to be a Major, although I reserve judgement on this for later deliberation; but I will state categorically that having a degree from a barber's college does not qualify you to practice medicine, nor more importantly, to determine what is and what is not a dead body."

This appeared to be an accusation to which the doctor was accustomed to responding for he stepped forward briskly saying, "I did not graduate from any barber college, I . . . " At this point the officer fingered the safety latch on his weapon, and where he walked demons wove a circle round him thrice. "Enough! This man is a complete charlatan. He doesn't even have a degree from a reputable barber's college, and the verminous swine is so contemptuous of us as to admit it. Now, Rutkowski, as one of the world's leading authorities on agriculture, and as a graduate of a reputable barber's college, I want you to look at these two specimens. Think carefully and grant us your professional opinion. Come, Rutkowski, what is it to be, tomatoes or squash?"

So I looked at them again, and sure enough, they were just frozen vegetables . . . squash.

THE SWEETEST SOUND OF ALL

We are in the shit. Two thogs have been hit by RPGs. They are using RPGs like the warehouse is just next door. Will someone please tell these guys they are supposed to be poorly armed. We are not maintaining fire superiority here.

I would like to speak to someone in the complaint department. In fact, I would like to kill someone in the complaint department.

Artillery is refusing the fire mission because they are informed by Battalion that there are friendlies in the impact area. Friendlies! We are the only friendlies I can find. No! We are no longer friendlies either.

Wait! I hear it. Sweet Jesus, the most beautiful sound in the world is coming our way. Thomp! Thomp! Thomp! Thomp! Salvation is at hand. There is no sound like it. The blades smash the air with determination and purpose as if they were clawing their way across the sky hand over hand.

They pass slow and steady overhead with green tracers playing around them. We open up with every thing we have to surppress the ground fire. Our positions are marked by smoke grenades. The pilot's voice sounds as sure as the guy at the McDonald's asking for your order. I love you. We love you. You are the sweetest sound in the world.

MENDELEVIUM, MESOTHORIUM, AND BEANS AND FRANKS

"Any of you guys got any mendelevium?" Said by Dimitri while searching inside his helmet liner on Hill 22. "Hey, any of you guys got any mendelevium?" Said louder by Dimitri on Hill 22.

"Frigg you, Dimitri, and your mesothorium." Said by Carruthers while finishing his breakfast of canned ham and eggs most foul.

"Carruthers, you unlearned shit, I speak of mendelevium, not mesothorium. Even under these vile conditions a man must nurture the higher organs and not fall prey to the loutish pursuits of the great unwashed multitude."

"You smell like shit, Dimitri." Said by Riley in the same foxhole with Dimitri on Hill 22. "Riley, I wouldn't deign to grace your existence by my attention. However, you don't happen to have any mendelevium, do you?" Said by Dimitri as he peers suspiciously at one of Riley's C-ration cans.

Riley grabs the C-ration can and sits on it. "No! I don't have your stinking mendelevium."

"Give me the mendelevium, you greasy Irish shit." Dimitri is reaching for his shoulder-holster-cooler-than-you-.45 that never fires more than one round without jamming.

Riley sits beatific with the radiant smile of the god who ate your canary. "Frigg you, Dimitri, this is my beans and franks, not your lousy mesothorium."

"Mendelevium, mendelevium, not mesothorium, you ass."
Garumph! Garumph! Death-flowers bloom in our garden of
concertina wire and landmines.

"Jesus-Frigging-Christ, the Cong are after the mesothorium!"
Screamed by Carruthers while digging a new foxhole in his
old foxhole.

"Mendelevium, you ass, mendelevium! We don't have any
damn mesothorium." Said by Dimitri while wrestling Riley
for the C-rats can. "Give them the damn can for Christ's
sake!" The death-flowers are blooming all over now. The
can sails high over the concertina wire. Rainbows and hum-
mingbirds made from broken razors watch it pass. Silence.
The death-flowers are gone. "That was my last can of beans
and franks, you bastard." Said by Riley as he attempts to
strangle Dimitri on Hill 22.

CRAZY BENJI

Crazy Benji is dead. Just like that. The world wasn't destroyed, it didn't turn blue, the stone didn't sing, no one spoke in tongues, there were no unusual apparitions in the night sky and my feet hurt as much now as when he was alive. I've been on patrol for three years with 200 pounds of extraneous garbage designed to camouflage me as an Army Surplus Store.

Benji was beautiful. He made things be, he could talk to anybody about anything, he had no reasons, he never made excuses, he'd steal anything from you, and he'd give you anything that belonged to him or anybody else. Yesterday he stole death when I wasn't looking. But my feet still hurt.

LYLE, HE-OF-THE-RED-MIST

Quiet! Let's just all be quiet. People are making a hell of a lot of racket around here.

I love patty-dikes. They make such nice homes. I am behind one now with Lyle. The water is very sweet and I am almost invisible. Can anyone see me? Hello? Hello?

I am sweating profusely. I am producing a great deal of water. I think I have urinated on myself and a few others. Let us forget it and be very quiet.

Quiet, Lyle, my sweet thing. We must be quiet. You must not breathe that way, Lyle, my love. It's so noticeable, Lyle. Everyone else is breathing clear and you are breathing a red mist.

Lyle, he-of-the-red-mist, do not try to speak. Be at peace for my M-16 shall comfort them. Soon I will lift up from our sanctuary and send death scurrying into yonder tree line to plague the little slope-headed shits once again. Are you listening to this, Lyle?

You must concentrate on listening, not breathing. You are scaring me, Lyle. Get a grip on yourself and stop that crap.

Don't point, Lyle. I can see the hole. What do you want me to do? I could yell, Corpsman! Corpsman! Lyle, are you listening? The Corpsman is right over there. Are you looking, Lyle? That's him with his pretty legs blown off. That was him screaming. He was screaming Corpsman! Corpsman! In the end he called upon himself, Lyle.

Lyle, you are a shit. Have I ever done this to you? Lyle! Lyle, what have you done? Lyle, where is your red mist? Lyle! Lyle, that's me poking you. Lyle! I've changed my mind. Lyle, you can breathe red mist if you want to.

Grandfather, what are you doing? Don't lie so quietly. Grandfather, you're scaring me. Grandfather, please come back. Who will make the fire in the big stove and tell me what to do?

Lyle, they're calling me. I've got to go, Lyle. Get your red mist back and I will return in a little while as soon as we've put paid to the slopes. Just rest here. I'm going to take your ammo. OK? OK?

Lyle, if you see my grandfather, tell him I need him and I love him. OK? OK?

THE RISING PRICE OF LACRAH

We are making a battalion sweep. It is a vacation sweep, a let-them-know-we-are-here sweep. Yesterday an announcement was printed in the Hated-Cong Daily News, invitations were sent to interested parties and the Goodyear blimp flew over the sweep area with electric sign blazing.

It is very early in the morning. The guys with the cymbals go first, then a twenty-four piece Marine Corps marching band follows, accompanied by a large, unidentified Mexican playing a calliope. Weapons beat against canteens, dog tags rattle, the engines of the thogs cough to life, and men mix fear with boredom, unable to decide what formula is appropriate.

About 1300, we are riding the thogs through a field of what appears to be stinkweed. The tracks of the thogs cut wide paths through the stinkweed which does not seem to mind. Suddenly two Vietnamese, a little old lady Vietnamese and a little old man Vietnamese, appear as if by magic standing in the field. They are near dead. They have scared us. Every weapon points a finger of fear in their direction.

They are held in time. Stop! They wisely remain still and silent. Then the fear is gone and only caution and curiosity remain. Suddenly they both begin to chatter and gesture toward the stinkweed. They pick up the plants we have destroyed with our tracks and make chewing motions while pointing to their mouths. Is the stinkweed a food?

Some Marines laugh. These are pogues who are new kids on our block. They are ignored and soon disappear. The rest of us listen respectfully. We do not understand, but we respect. What are they trying to tell us? They continue to make the chewing motions and now the old woman is pointing to the tree line. Does she want us to go around the field? It is impossible to explain that the thogs cannot negotiate the marshy terrain near the tree line.

The old man motions again, pointing to the stinkweed and saying, "Lacrah, Lacrah." We offer money. They refuse. We offer C-rats. They refuse and point toward the tree line. The old woman is crying and wailing. What is the cost of Lacrah?

We must go. There is no time left for understanding. We leave some money pinned to the ground with a tent peg. The old woman has a hoe. As the lead thog starts into motion, she smashes the hoe against the armored sides of the thog. The old man stands looking at the destroyed plants. Again and again the old woman strikes the thog as it moves gently forward. We do not look at her. No weapons are turned toward her. At a comfortable distance all eyes return to them. They are standing as we left them. Side by side in their field of Lacrah, they are judging us out of context with the tiny reality in which we hide.

The sweep goes on. We find no one and no one finds us. Two days of motion and waiting. Two days of impending fear and we are headed home. The field of Lacrah has been destroyed by our passing. The Vietnamese are gone. The money remains. Willy walks over to pick up the money. As he pulls on the peg, a mine goes off. Willy is thrown three yards away and the money falls like concrete around him. Each day we learn a little more about the price of Lacrah.

THE TRAITORS

The heat is like a great weight that you drag around in the dust behind you. Two thogs wait, making panting noises at the edge of the perimeter. The officer waits, and two 500 pound bombs, donated by the People's Air Force, wait some four klicks away.

The demolition man for whom we wait comes waddling toward the perimeter. He is a toad-person with things hanging all over him: C-4, fuses, other types of explosives, a grease gun and a few thousand rounds of ammunition. You'd think there was a war on.

He comes clanking up to the first thog and starts to climb on. The officer speaks. "Take the next thog back, it's a safer place." "Sir, I live with danger," states the demo man. "Well, live with it on the next thog," replies the officer and, so saying, sets the thog in motion.

About two hours later we find the bombs nestled in the soft earth waiting. We form a defensive perimeter. The demo-man sets to work. Twenty minutes later he asks the officer if he can detonate. The officer walks over and looks at the bombs. He touches the silver, shining, sterile workings of death waiting. He walks over to a patch of blue flowers about twenty feet from the bombs. "Will these flowers be destroyed?" "Yes sir, it'll blow everything within 150 yards straight to hell."

"I can't ask my comrades in the People's Marine Corps to go against their conscience. They aren't murderers. What kind of base brutes do you take us for who would knowingly annihilate one of God's most beautiful and harmless creations from this sullen earth?"

"We have to blow these damn things."
"I don't have to do shit, you enlisted son-of-a-bitch, and say sir when you are being disrespectful."
"Yes sir."
"Were you being disrespectful?"
"No sir."
"Then don't say sir when you are not being disrespectful, you homicidal son-of-a-bitch."

So we spend two hours digging up the blue flowers and moving them half a klick away. Two days later the lead thog hits a mine. The officer isn't scratched. He is never, ever scratched, but Crazy Bill buys a stone. We come back to where the blue flowers grow.

We pull the flowers up one by one. They are placed in a body bag and buried near a mostly destroyed Catholic church by *la rue sans joie*.

Tell the Lacedaemonians passerby
That here obedient to our fate we lie.
May 1, 1967
For their innocence cannot be excused
R. I. P.

BUT CAN YOU PLAY HERE?

We are soon dead. There will be no new sunrise. There are already many dead and wounded, but this is one great hill. You have got to come straight at us or fly. I love this damn place.

The radio is on. Johnny Unitas has come in to win the game. No shit here. No need for silence. No need for stealth. You want us, you got us. It's a damn good hill.

The weather is bad. No air support. The rain is like ball bearings with a purpose. Johnny U has just lost to the Jets. That cuts it for me.

I think we are about to lose, too. We won't get to play tomorrow. I would take you on a hill Johnny Unitas. Twenty stitches and still playing. The greatest compliment that can be given is, " I would take you on a hill."

I feel you know something else. There is no one I want to hit. I just want out of here with decency. I have already hit a lot of people I never even met. I think I'm about to be dead. No new set of downs.

They will come soon. They will pay dearly for this hill with no name. I'm ready to evolve. I'm ready to be something more. Hell! I'm ready to be anything. I'm down to twenty rounds and a wake up call. "Kill them all, let God sort them out." Is this all there is?

MEANINGLESS ORDERS, MEANINGLESS MINDS

He's a new-boy. He's a Major, but he's a new-boy. He's not going to do well. You can tell by the number of meaningless orders he gives. He's nervous. We are talking ten meaningless orders a minute here.

Lighten the hell up. Give us a chance and we'll teach you the ropes. Just lighten up and give us a chance. He's complained that no one has a regulation haircut. He's complained that we have unauthorized weapons. He's complained of a certain lack of military discipline. He's complained that we have unauthorized markings on our thogs. He's given the officer twenty orders in the last ten minutes. The officer has politely passed these on to the Gunny, who has politely ignored them.

The Major sits across from the officer in our lovely bunker. The Major is cleaning his cooler-than-you .45. The officer is reading "the book" *The White Goddess*. We have all sneaked a peek . Some heavy shit. The Gunny is making up the guard duty roster. Jesus! I love that man.

Bang! It's amazing the noise a .45 makes in an enclosed area. The round hits about two inches right of the officer's head. The officer doesn't even look up, "Bitch pulls a bit to the left, Major." "Shit," says the Gunny as he gets up and removes the .45 from the Major's hand. "The Gunny is going to tune that baby up a might. Right, Gunny?" "Shit," says the Gunny as he removes the firing pin from the Major's cooler-than-you .45 caliber non-government issue pistol.

WAITING

We are waiting, lying quiet in a moon empty night. The magic L for ambush has been made across the trail and sometime soon, shadow spinning, the Hated-Cong will come. Like smiles mixed with honey, they will come.

We are waiting, lying quiet in a moon empty night. Fear spreads over me and embraces the fear of my comrades in the night. Our fear is like the giggles of little girls at their first prom. It will run on, a living thing apart, until it is struck by a larger reality. For now, it is all my reason to be.

We are waiting, lying quiet in a moon empty night. I have for those around me a love I will never have for you. Even those for whom we wait are loved more than you. I have always been just here and I always will be here in a moon empty night.

A tiny noise comes. Then three claymores flash, shredding flesh and bone. Flares make a day and night of shadows that paint clown faces on both dead and living. I am firing at targets of opportunity.

We are waiting, lying quiet in a moon empty night. I snuggle into the returning cocoon of darkness. The smells have changed. There is cordite, burn and blood within my mind.

I lust for the laughter of daylight. Just let me get home and I will never run away again.

GREEN SMOKE MORNING

It's a green smoke morning. My feet are alive and screaming. My mouth is a crematorium for two million cigarettes.

I am watching green smoke in the distance. It moves leisurely toward the position held by the Hated-Cong. It moves toward them as if curious to see what manner of beast would disturb our morning revelry. Overhead the jets await their call to life.

"Lightning One, this is Animals Actual. Target from green smoke, 350 meters north, tree line, troops in same. Do you copy? Over."
"Animals Actual, Lightning One copies. Over."
"Lightning One, make one dummy pass to be sure you don't roast the wrong ass. Over."
"Lightning One, will do. Starting run. Out."

Yes, sweet Jesus, once again in air conditioned comfort they come to roast the heathen. Tremble all ye without adequate air defense for the hour of destruction is upon thee and neither thy rod nor thy staff will comfort thee.

Listen to that sound. God's chariot, like a necklace of thunder-claps, passes over and fulfills his prophecy of flame. God! I love that sound. I am safe within its walls and mine enemy trembles. Mine enemy beshits himself. Mine enemy is scared shitless. Get yours, I've had mine.

There is still enough fear in this bunker left over from the night to fill the Grand Canyon. There is just barely enough room left for my radio man to be scared. The ass is pushing my fear with his fear. My fear pushes back, pulling rank and forcing his little fear into a corner where it sits whimpering and demanding more air strikes.

THE PRISONER

He rests against the track of a thog. His right hand is tied to the track. The Corpsman is wrapping C-rat box wire around the prisoner's mangled left forearm. It has been splintered by a .50 caliber round.

We have given him a cigarette. It hangs loosely from his lips. He does not whine or scream. His face is contorted with pain, but he makes no noise. Would I be so brave?

Each of us wonders what he would do in the same situation. Every effort is made to comfort our foe. He seems so small, so very small. He is as small as each of us feels when the fear is upon us. We reach to comfort him from our own demons.

It is not always the same. Today we have taken no casualties, killed five of them, and taken one prisoner. We hold the only high ground for six klicks, we have tanks and tracks, the sky is full of friendlies on call, and we are within easy reach of four batteries of artillery. There is time left over to feel our own humanity. The beast within each of us is fed. The best time to be a prisoner is when the other side has won.

IT'S JUST A PICTURE

It's just a picture. I can't remember thinking much of it before. My mother and father are standing beside their new car. They are holding my hand. My parents are very young and attempting to look foolish. I am so young I cannot remember.

The picture is in my upper left pocket. I am covered with blood. I have given every order I need to give. We have won. Nothing important will happen soon.

A thog beside me burns. Three Hated-Cong are her companions. They have been moved out of her sight that she may die in peace. They have been harmed no more.

Next to me my radioman sleeps. He has been awake thirty-six hours. I cannot remember when I have been awake.

I am covered with blood. I have given every order I need to give. We have won. I sleep inside a picture held by two giant hands.

THE SALUTE

A night most foul. The rain shark savages the world and sneaks beneath my poncho for morsels of dry flesh.

We are in the port of Da Nang, the big "D". LST's lay like beached steel whales upon the sand. In some are heard the noise of Boom-Boom girls plying their trade. There are twenty of us and no one even looks interested. We have been in-country too long and we are tired to death of the whole damn thing.

We have come to pick up four new thogs and accompanying equipment. They have traveled the great ocean to reinforce our cause. God bless them one and all.

Four great, green thogs have brought us. They are silver-backs who have known heat, rain, hard travel, wounds, and blood. The new thogs seem to huddle together for protection inside the gut of the LST. Be kind, old ones, for once you too were only steel and currant without soul.

I have inspected the thogs to make sure they are ready for their run back home to Hill 55. The Gunny is in the LST checking out the new thogs and stealing the Navy blind. Soon the morning will break upon us and we must be on our way.

I walk into the maw of the LST. "Detail, attennnnhut!" Before I can stop myself, I have brought my weapon up and flipped the safety catch. The Gunny is standing ramrod straight and saluting someone. Is General Westmoreland here? Is he after the Boom-Boom girls?

The Gunny knew Jesus when He was a corporal. They served

in Korea together ("Now there was a real war!"). He has four Bronze Stars and three Purple Hearts.

Fifteen other Marines are standing ramrod straight. Dirt, grime, and time in-country are woven into them. "Sir! The Gunny wishes to report four thogs and accompanying equipment ready for transfer." Five Navy types have also come to attention including two Lieutenants.

I also note there are three Marines missing. Somewhere Navy supplies and equipment are changing hands.

SNIPES EAT PAYDAY
CANDY BARS

Hill 55 is still standing. Wishing does not make things come true. I am still in it, on it and around it. Also here are dust and sun and centipedes twelve feet long. There is much fear and boredom.

I have come out from under my rock and am sunning myself. I am lying on top of a log cabin buried in the ground. These are all the rage on Hill 55.

The snipes are lying on top of a bunker. They are having a party. There are Oreo cookie wrappers and empty Spam cans all over the place. All the snipes are inside a huge giggle squatting on the bunker.

There is a little snipe looking through a spotter scope that is looking deep into the valley floor. Another snipe is lying motionless with his Remington pointed into the valley. Far away in the valley two tiny shapes are moving. The snipe squeezes ever so gently and a tiny projectile is born running. The projectile is running straight and true toward one of the tinys in the valley.

The snipe with the Remington has his soft hat turned backwards like a U-Boat commander. The tiny victims were unaware of U-Boats in these waters. The snipes are giggling. Another ship has been sent to the bottom.

Their giggles are expanding inside the big giggle they live in and I am afraid of an explosion. This doesn't occur because the snipes are settling down now to watch the sinking victim. They take turns looking through the periscope. They are waiting for the other tiny, who has gone to ground, to try to rescue his comrade.

They wait in vain. The other tiny does not return for his friend. Now the paperwork begins. The snipes must record the date, the estimated yardage to target, the type of target, weather conditions, ammunition expended, the number of confirmed kills and possibles, and the number of PayDay candy bars expended. All of this information is kept in a great, blue ledger.

The ledger is two feet by two feet. It is embellished with gold and all entries are made with a quill pen. Many tinys could hide in this book, but only their numbers live there.

Snipes are magic people. There is a desperate magic about being able to reach out unseen across space and time with death on your finger. They giggle because they fear their own magic, because they know they are forever imprisoned by it. Sometimes I giggle with them. Sometimes a giggle just leaps out before I can stop it, but I never allow one to come home again.

64

THE GREAT WHITE WHALE

The Khobi Ton Ton valley lies quiet and flat for fifteen square miles until it rushes skyward making mountains. There is a seething mob of mountains that look disdainfully upon Hill 62. The hill has been cast out from its brethren to sit squat and lonely in the valley floor. There is a company of Marines who sit squat and lonely with it.

Their positions are resupplied and supported by a platoon of thogs. From the hill top you can watch them winding slowly across the valley floor carrying food, water and ammunition.

They are great, ugly beasts, but they are beautiful to see when you are hungry, or the Hated-Cong are upon you, and they come hurling balls of death amongst them. The officer is their master. He and Captain Babs, our CO, have long ago established a quarrel on which to brood.

After the quarrel began we started receiving messages in the C-rats boxes—messages like "Captain Ahab has a wooden leg." Soon Captain Babs was known as Captain Ahab. Later we began to get messages saying, "Screw Captain Ahab" signed by the Great White Whale. This went on for months and Captain Ahab grew more sullen and remote. Sometimes he asked for Queequeg and demanded we man the long boats.

On January 6, 1967 at 0230 one of the outposts reported a great white shape moving solemnly into the valley floor. The Captain was called. The great white shape circled Hill 62 making noises like a whale blowing water through its hole. The Captain was heard to say "Avast thar," before he went to hide in his bunker.

The next morning in the valley floor spelled out in flattened rice plants was "Screw Captain Ahab"— signed, the Great White Whale. That afternoon they took Captain Ahab away in one of the long boats.

THE MANY AND THE FEW

Newspaper men, like buzzards, circle to ensure there is no danger. When they appear, you can feel the despise sitting heavy in the air. There is a smell upon them and they are cursed.

Their stories are written in back areas, bars and houses of whore. Some, however, are different. These are few and respected as one of us. These few always seem sad. They wait for something to unravel the complex madness they have known. There is a quiet bravery about them that does not have to be spoken or written. They are few.

The many wait for a carnage of mistakes or theatrical nonsense to feed upon. They lie even when they write the truth. They steal our reality and their own, and they never spell our names right.

WHISPER FOR THE DEAD

We are alive. Morning soon comes. Half-light snuggles among us. I feel as if I am holding myself for comfort.

Upon Hill 22 there is a chaos of discarded, maimed things. It is a landscape suitable only for the night. Only the dead seem comfortable.

This is their home now as it never was before. The rest of us are intruders. They are gentlemen. There is no pointing and giggling, no quick, ugly remarks. There is only a too gracious silence.

They lay where death found them. Each rests at exactly the right place in space and time. In the moments of dying we saw only chaos. Now the perfection is obvious.

We whisper. We are out of place. We do not wish to offend. We are alive.

THE LAUNDRY MAN

Suddenly, most suddenly, as a waterfall turned upon the watchers below, it becomes. The bastards are trying to kill me. An RPG has struck the right track. We are a one legged beast going nowhere. I depress the iron butterfly on the .50 and I am enveloped in a joyous surge of noise. The Hated-Cong are so busy watching the sound and hugging the earth that their shots are erratic and forlorn. Death as big as a house. Yes, sweet Jesus, let it fall upon them.

Delicious! What a delicious noise I am making. Trees are being smashed and the Hated-Cong are surely dying in yonder treeline. My lovely noise ends. I must reach down into the innards of my great beast for another case of my magic pellets. I am stooping, reaching, when a shadow covers the hatch. Death's shadow is upon me.

There is an entrenching tool wedged between two sandbags at the bottom of the thog. There is a whir of magic and the entrenching tool is flashing upwards cleaving the skull of mine enemy. He disappears like a flash of white fish belly back beneath the surface of the pond. A grenade explodes harmlessly against the armor on the side of the thog. He was a small one, Maude, so we threw him back.

In five minutes it is over. They have gone wherever they go and we are policing the area. We cannot find my shadow or my entrenching tool. Later we find he wasn't a Hated-Cong at all, just a guy named Harry who wanted to give me a laundry ticket, but he was too late.

SEAN O'DIEM

He died on Monday, of peeking. Just an eye above the patty dike, dear mom, for one last look around. Where shall we find you tomorrow?

I must search his sweet body for secrets to end the war. This could be it. Yes sir, right here on this poor dead son-of-a-bitch, the ultimate secret could reside. Do the Hated-Cong have the bomb?

His pockets contain loose ammunition, lint, a collection of baseball cards, and a wallet made in Saigon. The wallet has the secret.

Hidden in a corner of the wallet is a shamrock encased in plastic. Could this be the legendary Lug-of-the-Red-Branch? Are the Hated-Cong using Irish mercenaries? Was the shamrock taken from a dead Irishman? Are the Hated-Cong secretly fighting in Northern Ireland? Is there no end to English perfidy?

This evidence must be immediately forwarded to Battalion. Only our superiors—men who have spent their lives delving into just such problems—can answer questions of this nature. Good night Sean O'Diem, wherever you may be.

RELIGIOUS RITES

I am watching an olive drab bulldozer push eighty-two bodies into a trench. We have taken their weapons and all else that belonged to them—all else that could be buried in such a place. I am reminded of pictures from other wars. The pictures are superimposed upon my vision.

They died last night outside our perimeter. Not one made it inside. It was utter stupidity. It was some bizarre religious ritual with dancing, speaking in tongues, confessions and sacrifices. Many, many sacrifices lie here. You stupid shits.

I was here too. I was forced to participate and I enjoyed it. I enjoyed it so much I could scream forever. They are lemmings. Lemmings who have come to fertilize the soil. Each year for the past two years they have come in July to make their sacrifice. In year one, twenty-one filled the trenches. In year two, thirty-eight filled the trenches. Now there are eighty-two. None of the scrubby foliage inhabiting the area has taken any appreciable notice. I, however, believe in them. There will come a time some time soon when the sacrifice will tell. I feel that next year the magic number will be reached, but I will be home and all of this will only be a picture from an old book of half-remembered wars. You stupid shits.

#32

There are souls in steel. Each thog has its own. If you are with them long enough, if you sweat and bleed with them, you will know. I do not know if all machines have souls, but I know these do. Each has a distinct personality, as distinct as the men who ride them.

Maybe it is because we depend on one another so. Maybe it is the blood of Marines and Hated-Cong that have drained into their bilges, mingling in death to give life to creatures of steel.

The soul of # 32 was the largest of all. She was a warrior and a comrade. Each day she gave her all. No complaints. No questions. No looks of implied guilt. She was one of us.

Two years in-country and no R&R. Two years in-country and every task was done. She died on September 7, 1967. Three RPGs. Each hit a death blow and still she fought.

She died well. She held us beneath her steel wings until the end. We shall not forget you # 32.

NO MORE CLOWNS

The woman takes a good picture. She is sitting on an anti-aircraft gun somewhere in Hanoi. She is pretty in a tinsel, plastic-coated-for-your-protection fashion. Her face holds a vacuous smile demanding some intense, identifying cause to fill up her empty time.

She kills her thousands with the jawbone of an ass. Those she has harmed seem strangely unaffected. Eighteen year old Marines know ignorance when it is thrust upon them. Do they not suffer boot lieutenants every day of their lives?

We are embarrassed. The Hated-Cong are embarrassed. We are sad for her. They are sad to use her, but there is a war on. The picture will not be hung on their walls, and their children will hear no stories of the strange woman from America. It is just one more hole in the Process that had to be filled.

This war is ours. She is a dilettante of chaotic direction. You must pay and play, or get your silly ass out. We just don't have time to chit-chat. We are the evil that grown-ups do, and we need no more clowns for we have a sufficiency of clowns.

THE INDIAN

I hate the Indian. I hate him so much it fogs my eyes up and I can't see to hate him. I hate the Indian because he isn't afraid of anything. He doesn't know anything and he smiles all the time like he knows something you'll never find out. When the firing starts and everyone else is full of fear, he just smiles.

His smile sits around. Sometimes I find it in my foxhole. The other day it was sitting on the four-holer. One day I'm going to kill that son-of-a-bitch.

Once he was twenty yards to my right when we got ambushed from the left flank. A real downpour. When I laid down I couldn't see to fire because the Indian had gotten all the way around in front of me. I started to shoot him in the ass, but his smile was there so I didn't. Then once he saved my life. He's dangerous.

Last night I was going to kill him. I was going to kill him because I couldn't stand to see him die. I just couldn't stand it and if he wasn't such a jerk he could understand that. He just can't stay out of harm's way. God! I hate that damn Indian.

SERUTAN E. DELGADO

Considering the magnitude of cosmic ray bombardment, it is highly unlikely that I will live to regret any of my previous actions. I would like, however, to take this opportunity to purge myself of an ongoing transgression. I am presently living with a 78 year old nymphomaniac named Serutan E. Delgado of the famous Puntain family Delgados. This woman believes herself to be a DC-6 cargo plane once flown over the Burma Hump by Terry and the Pirates. Although much used and weary with the weight of many flights, she insists on carrying me to the war every morning.

I shall never allow this to happen again because of the magnitude and because of the beastly noise she makes when she takes off.

HILL 55

It is dark and lonely on Hill 55 tonight. It was much the same last night. It is silent too, except for the occasional clank of metal on metal.

It is quiet because we are not allowed to speak. If we speak the Hated-Cong will know we are here. Of course, the fact that we have been mortared every other day, sniped at every day and attacked in force about every three months would lead you to believe the slopes already have some idea of our location. Maybe Battalion feels the Hated-Cong have grossly impaired short term memory.

"Jesus-Frigging-Christ." Said by Private Harrison as something furry runs over his boot.
"Who said that? Who is the son-of-a-bitch that screamed?" Screamed by the officer.
"Sir," whispered by Harrison.
"Nobody screams on this hill but officers. Speak up, damn it." Screamed by the officer.
"Private Harrison, sir," screamed by Harrison.
"Are you screaming Harrison, you enlisted son-of-a-bitch? Wait a minute. Gunny did you make Harrison an officer?" Asked by the officer.
"Shit no." Said by the Gunny.
"I knew it. I knew you weren't enough of an ass to be an officer, Harrison, and if I wasn't scared shitless of getting out of this hole, I would come over there and kill you."

THE THANKSGIVING NIGHT
MASSACRE

It is Thanksgiving and we have extra onions with our C-rats. For dinner I have canned ham and eggs with cranberry sauce. I am thankful for two things—a hot coke and no one is blatantly trying to kill me. The officer gives a speech thanking the Kennedys for starting such a nice little war and PayDay candy bars and Underwood Deviled Ham for making it bearable.

Before bed, I sit by the fireplace with mom and sister Sally recalling warm times from childhood past. We eat candied apples and say dull, happy things. I pet my shaggy dog and lick his face. As I go beddy-bye, contentment sits on my belly like a large jockey on a small horse.

Mom's screams wake me in the middle of my night. We both run for the slit-trench to give company to the .50 caliber machinegun. Sister Sally is there already. Dad picks up his old accordion and lays into the Beer Barrel Polka. God! I love that song.

Two Hated-Cong wearing pilgrim outfits appear at the wire with a Bangalore Torpedo disguised as a large turkey. The turkey explodes. The wire remains. The Cong are confettied. About forty Cong appear on the right flank wearing loin cloths, feathered headdresses, and moccasins. They are not carrying peace pipes. Later, when it is all over, the officer passes among the Thanksgiving Day revellers. He says there is a great lesson to be learned. "Never spend Thanksgiving night with an Oriental."

THE ECONOMIC FACTOR

If all goes well, we will be home for Christmas. We will be home because of Wilson Byron Fogswill, Private First Class.

Wilson had two years of economics at Harvard. He tells everyone this fact. He also tells everyone how much money can be made doing this or that. If money could be made by boring people, Wilson would be a rich man today.

Wilson found a statistic indicating that it costs the American tax payer $85,452.35 to kill a single North Vietnamese soldier or Hated-Cong. This is an economic tragedy in Wilson's opinion. His suggestion is to cut out the middle man.

Instead of spending American resources, we simply pay old Ho Chi to kill them. If the American government pays Ho $30,000 per soldier executed, there is an individual item savings of $55,452.35.

Two weeks ago Wilson sent a letter to Ho with the details of his proposal. Yesterday he received a reply. Ho is offering to execute his own soldiers for $65,000 each. Wilson is conferring with Battalion concerning a counter proposal. Soon a new offer will be forwarded to Ho.

Last night we did $1,025,428.20 worth of business on Hill 22. We do not know how much it cost to kill the three Marines. Wilson is investigating this and none of us likes the look in his eye.

DO YOU LIKE GREEKS?

Someone has put shrapnel in my legs. I feel dizzy and nauseous. I want to go home. A great green locust with rubber wheels comes for me and others waiting. During the flight I have a projectile vomiting contest with a trooper who has lost four fingers of his left hand. He wins, but I step on his remaining finger and steal one of his Joe DiMaggio baseball cards.

At Charlie Med we are treated with all the tenderness of a returning band of gypsies in a small Southern town. I am taken into a room to see someone they claim is a doctor. I am not handcuffed.

They have cut my boots off. There is blood on the floor. The doctor has on a flack jacket, a red pair of shorts and shower shoes. He looks at me suspiciously. "Do you have any cigarettes?" I give him a Camel. He reaches into his flack jacket for a lighter. He bends over and cups his hand as if a wind was blowing and lights up. Jesus, where do they find these people?

"Do you like Greeks?" As he asks this, he peers intently into my eyes. I spend a few minutes vowing my eternal love for all things Greek. After all of this he says one word. "Good!" Somehow he makes this an entire paragraph. There is a long pause while he takes out a lead pipe and absentmindedly pounds it into his palm.

"You know my brother, Alexy?" Before I can answer, he nods and goes on, "Of course, he is a great neurosurgeon, but where are the great patients of the great neurosurgeon?" Here he looks at me as if I may have stolen them. The loss of blood has ruined my memory, consequently I am afraid to deny it. It could be.

The doctor gets up and begins to pace back and forth, his flack jacket fluttering over his red shorts like great green bat wings. "You are certain you love the Greek people?" Then he walks behind me and there is an explosion of darkness. I awake elsewhere.

I awake to a large nose peering at me. "Good!" Another paragraph spoken. I have the feeling I have met the great Alexy.

SNAPSHOTS

In a picture history of World War II there is a photo of a German soldier who has just been shot. He rests cantilevered in midair, his rifle falling from his outstretched hand.

Does his mother have this photo in her wallet? "Yes, Hilda darling, this is my son Helmut. That boy, such a character, spends all of his time in midair dying. Can't get him home to eat for the world."

And today, near Hill 22, we are taking pictures of old Ho Kai. Ho is lying behind a rice paddy dike with most of his skull missing forever. We shot Ho and two acquaintances trying to cross an open area in broad daylight. What could Ho and friends have been thinking? What mission sent them out with reckless abandon into a daylight world of Marines?

Sitting in our tree line, we watched with disbelief as Ho and his companions emerged from the opposite tree line making small, happy sounds. Were they discussing the weather, or the Dodgers' chances for the pennant, or the alarming absence of Marines in the area? What led them to believe we weren't around? Is their intelligence officer as big a moron as ours? My God! Is it possible we have the same one?

We were mystified as we watched their progress. Had someone left a trail of bread crumbs? We could have tried to capture them, but we are old men at this trade.

It is 1700 hours and time to go home before we turn into pumpkins. If you just blast away, maybe you will get one WIA who can talk. One who will be uninterested in further conflict.

We have requested a British officer from Battalion to help fulfill their demands for prisoners. Stepping out in starched tunic, ramrod straight, not a fly on him, spit-shined boots, and not a drop of sweat in sight. "I say, chaps, you are surrounded. Best give up and live to fight another day. Bad luck and all that rot." Salutes smartly and breaks into a chorus of "Only Mad Dogs and Englishmen" as the wogs gratefully form a column of ones and march themselves into captivity.

The rounds from two machineguns struck Ho. He hung in midair. Now he is a snapshot too. "Three Viet-Cong irregulars KIA at 1700 hours near Doc Lo II, 754108625. Three AK-47s, one map, one landmine (antipersonnel), one basketball (deflated), and one snapshot of Helmut dying."

THE REAL

I'm eating cheese C-rats, John Wayne crackers, and onions. I have come to love onions because they are so real. Things from tin cans and plastic are part of the war effort. When we are killed, they bag us in green plastic and ship us home.

Now each of us is equipped with a square of green plastic at the base of our skulls. When we die, the square explodes. The deceased is enveloped in a green body bag with name, rank and serial number stenciled thereon. God bless them all.

Now you know why I love onions. Stubby, the comshaw, gets them for us, and we eat them for him. They swell in your mouth with amazing taste and live there a long time. The air is full of the breath of them.

The war is nowhere near as real. I never really look at it. I have noticed that those who do look start screaming . . . and they never stop. You can't always hear them, but they never stop anyway.

No one looks at death either. We have heard about it, but we seldom look. Sometimes.

FREEDOM

"So they can be free, that's why, you stupid shit. All we are trying to do is make the little gook bastards free to choose whatever they want."

"So what if they choose not to be free?"

"Everybody wants to be free, wants to walk the earth at his own pace, free to stop and rest forever if he chooses, free to worship or not to worship. No one chooses not to be free."

"Sarge, can I get R&R next month? I haven't had a day in ten months."

"Christ no, you moron. You think you can just walk the earth at your own pace, leave when you choose? Try it and I'll put your ass in a sling."

THE SILVER BULLET

"They're not firing silver bullets are they?" Said unnoticed by Corporal Stamm during a fire-fight near Con Thien.

"Are the bastards firing silver bullets?" And the war goes on. Isiah receives a .30 caliber round that sends him far away.

"Did anyone see that bullet? Was that a silver bullet?" The Hated-Cong are proving excessive in their response. We have caught them in a green-valley-place-to-die.

"That's the only thing that will kill me." Said partially unnoticed down the way.

"The bastards are firing silver bullets. Keep your heads down." Said almost completely noticed by the officer. He was right, too, because Corporal Stamm is hit just as he leans over to hear what the officer is saying. They get him with a silver bullet and an old wadded up poem by e. e. cummings.

SWEET DEATH BY MAIL

Life and death come through the mail. "Dear John, I am betraying you today because you are fighting an unpopular war, because you aren't here and Billy is, and because I can no longer remember any reason not to betray you." Let's go out and kill one for Mary Jane.

You can be bullet proof when the madness overcomes you. Wheeling the great sword overhead, berserk in a night of despair, let us cleave the heads of the little heathen brutes. God! It would be good to get your hands on a tiny Hated-Cong and crush his skull. Failing that, let us beat the shit out of whoever comes along looking happy.

Do you know I can't even remember what the bitch looks like? Do you know I'm lying? Do you know I have looked at that picture five million times? I want something to hold onto that is not in-country, something that is mine to hold onto even if it is not true. Why didn't she just frigging lie? Jesus H. Christ!

The Hated-Cong know. They are hiding. They think I'll cool off in a couple of days and they'll be back. Wrong! Wrong! Wrong!

I'm carrying the letter with me and I read it anytime I'm feeling good, then I'm mad as hell again. Jesus! The pain is delicious. I am a child with a four pound loose tooth to worry back and forth in my mind. The pain is so sweet I could scream. Send me another one, you bitch.

THE WITCH DOCTOR

Every Sunday at 0700 we used to go to Hill 62. We didn't go to carry supplies or help in a fire-fight. We went because of Chaplin Quickford. The Chaplin said those boys were stuck in the middle of no place with the devil at their heels. No one else thought so. The officer especially didn't think so.

The first time the Chaplain came in to the bunker at 0430, the officer told him to get out because the war didn't start til 0630. Then Major Hemhurst called and ordered the officer to go. The officer called the sentry post and told them he was Major Hemhurst, and if anybody tried to leave the perimeter before 1100 hours they had better shoot the son-of-a-bitch, or he would have their ass in a sling. We didn't go that day, but the Major got wise and we started going regularly.

Every time we went, the Chaplain would try to make friends with the officer.
"Beautiful day."
"You can't cook worth a shit."
"I'm not a cook, I'm a chaplain."
"Why do you pretend to be a cook?"
"I never pretended to be a cook."
"At least you could pretend, you worthless bastard." The officer walked away from the Chaplain with a very pronounced limp, then stopped and looked back. When the officer resumed walking, his limp disappeared. Turning on the Chaplain, the officer screamed, "You lying toad, I knew you were a cook. If I wanted to get rid of my limp I would have said so." But the Chaplain had run away.

The war went on. Sometimes we thought the officer had him.

Like the time he put the dirty pictures in the prayer books. The Chaplain recovered. For two weeks the officer was exceptionally nice to the Chaplain. We waited.

Sunday we carried the Chaplain up to Hill 62. The officer had ordered fourteen rolls of barbed wire. It completely filled the thogs. There wasn't any place for the Chaplain to sit except with the barbed wire. The officer found every bump and gully. Somehow it took an extra hour to reach our destination. Little pricks of red and torn cloth was how the Chaplain was dressed when we got to Hill 62.

The Chaplain should have realized something was wrong when the officer and all the thog people sat down in the little area where the service was held. Such an event had not happened before, but the Chaplain was dazed from his bout with the barbed wire.

The Chaplain stood on the knoll where the service was held and reached into the box in which he carried the sacrament. He pulled out what he found and held it up in the morning sunlight. It was a chicken with its head cut off. The Chaplain gasped. The officer stepped closer looking at the chicken and shaking his head. "You heathen son-of-a-bitch. I'm going to tell Major Hemhurst you are practicing black magic . . . but you can keep my limp." And he did, too.

SCLAP METAL

Come, mother, and walk with me in the jungle demilitarized. It is green and sweet in our valley. Here in the Zone Demilitarized we are marching to our different drummer.

A tentative shot. An avalanche follows. The cheating little bastards. No one is supposed to be here. The mendacity of it is unrelenting.

The officer is screaming orders. You can hear the son-of-a-bitch forever. He is lying beside a tree stump and living in a movie. He is changing magazines when it happens. Out of the jungle waddles a yellow apparition of tatters, a Japanese army uniform made from moth's wings, in his hands a samurai sword and overlooking all, teeth of buck and hornrimmed eyes. He stumbles toward the officer, half a league, half a league onward. The yellow apparition reaches him. Bonsai! The sword falls across the officer's neck and disintegrates into a confetti storm of rust. The samurai waddles back into the jungle. And from the jungle comes a call, "Rousy Amelican sclap metal."

THE SASQUATCH TRAVELING
EMPORIUM

Every day at 1300 hours the war in the Khobi Ton Ton valley comes to an end. War's-End lasts until 1600 hours when hostilities are promptly resumed.

War's-End was the officer's idea. He talked with his opposite number with the Hated-Cong and soon the Sasquatch Traveling Emporium was born. At 1300 hours the thogs roll down into the center of the valley and set up shop. The shops offer candy bars, toothbrushes, soap, prophylactics, comic books, and all the things that make wars worth fighting.

The officer continues to introduce new products. Last month he sold Diem, his opposite number, on the idea of outfitting his entire battalion with new shoes. The officer pointed out the inferior quality of the tennis shoes worn by the Hated-Cong: how easily they rot, how foolish grown men look in tennis shoes and the unlikely possibility they would ever be drafted by an NBA team. Then the officer brought out what he described as the latest in modern American combat footwear - the solid steel GI boot.

The benefits are obvious: wears virtually forever, chrome covered to prevent rust, you can shave in it, and kick the shit out of anyone. The officer explained that the reason we weren't wearing them is because Diem was being given the benefit of a pre-inventory sale. Diem and his men went happily in their new footwear clanking off into the jungle to marvel at the stupidity of capitalist salesmen.

Later the officer pointed out the poor taste involved in the design of the Hated-Cong's helmets. The officer had two well known interior decorators discuss the appalling lack of taste with Diem. Diem was obviously chagrined and felt he had lost face due to his superiors' lack of foresight in designing helmets. Luckily the officer had an immediate solution— the concrete helmet.

The helmets the officer showed Diem were actually the bowls from concrete birdbaths. Turned upside down, however, they did make fine helmets. Again the benefits are obvious: virtually impervious to the worst monsoon rain, a whole battalion crouched in the open simply looks like a field of large mushrooms to American aircraft, wears forever, doubles as a wash basin, and can easily withstand the impact of .30 calibre slugs. Once again the terms were very generous and Diem and his men went clank-stoop into the jungle.

Two weeks later the officer sold Diem on the idea of placing a bicycle aerial with an identity flag on the top of each concrete helmet. This, of course, allowed Diem to recognize his men at great distances and facilitated proper control of forces in a combat situation.

We have virtually retired from the war here on Hill 55. If the Hated-Cong move, we know immediately. There is a vast clanking and waving of luminous identification flags preceding every operation. The steel boots leave a trail even a blind man could follow and the aftershave lotion the officer foisted on them will tingle the olfactory senses up to 600 yards.

There is only one great danger left. If you attack them when they are dug in on a hill, you are in for trouble. The weight of concrete birdbaths and steel boots rolling down a hill is awesome.

Here on top of Hill 55 we have placed a sign.
"Secured by Yankee ingenuity, steel boots, concrete birdbaths,
bicycle aerials, and aftershave. Make economics, not war."

THE RIDER

There was one of him on a bicycle peddling. He had an AK-47 slung across his back. The road was feather-flakes of earth raised six feet above the surrounding fields of grass.

A company of Marines lay sprinkled in the elephant grass. For two weeks the area had been declared a free-fire zone in which only citizens of the People's Marine Corps were allowed by official decree to exist. For two weeks we had searched in fits and spasms only finding nothing.

The rider's shape was melted and, reformed by the heat, wandering away from the surface of the road. Every eye was on him. From my pack I took a white helicopter marking panel and made upon it squares of black.

Just as he passed, I stepped out and waved the checkered flag of victory. Pandemonium broke loose. Rifles and C-rations were thrown into the air. The great John Phillips Sousa Memorial Seven Day Bicycle Race had ended.

The winner seemed astounded by his victory. He reached for his AK-47 and fell from glory. We buried him in the winner's circle in the middle of the road of feather-flake brown stretched tight across the Khobi Ton Ton valley.

Lin Doc Tho
Winner of the
John Phillip Sousa Memorial
Seven Day Bicycle Race
Ride In Peace
July 7, 1967

THE PROCESS

The road is infested with travelers. A Marine company infests either side of the road. Somewhere a decision is being made, a fortune cookie is being opened, the I Ching is consulted and a bathroom door closes.

Ragged buses made from broken mirrors, your grandfather's suspenders and false teeth totter past. Before each bus departs, a contest is held by Yale sophomores to see how many people, chickens, shopping bags, microwave ovens, and Ferris wheels can be stuffed into it. A circus of noise and confusion fills each bus. Bits and pieces are scattered beside the road.

We watch the people on the road. They watch us. We are spectators of one another. Each of us waits for the other to do something perfectly hilarious.

We are part of a process. The Process started many years ago although scholars differ as to the exact date. It is important only to realize that it does exist and it keeps us all here spectating each other. Even death is a spectator event. There is their-death and our-death and every spectator knows the difference.

A lady on a bicycle looks nasty at me. I don't care, but I look back and move my weapon threateningly in her direction. I do this only because I am part of the Process and I can't find a way to do anything else. I would like to smile, stop her, give her a Cadillac convertible, tell her my fears, listen to her fears, eat dinner with her parents and exchange gifts of understanding.

I cannot because I am part of the Process, and she is part of the Process, and because I do not wish to appear foolish even unto death.

ENVY

I envy him. He doesn't know because he is dead. He is lying behind a patty dike. The upper left portion of his skull is missing. There is a hole in his side and his leg. A .30 caliber machinegun is crumpled beneath him. I do not envy him for any of these reasons.

I envy him because of the girl. She is beautiful and she is dead. She is amazingly effeminate even in death, even with the large hole in her chest, even with the dirt, even with the bad smell, even with the mangled ammunition belt wrapped around her small hand.

I would like to take my knife and cut her into small pieces. I would like to feel the blade against her flesh and bone. I would like to kill and maim the stupidity of all this shit forever.

She did not leave him. Hope was long since gone. He was dead and she stayed waiting to die holding his hand. I have made him dead and tonight in our sleep when he least suspects, when he has grown to love me too, I shall kill him again and have my way with his woman. Later I will let her die, but she will never smell bad again.

SHARING

There is a honeysuckle rain falling. I am sitting on the steps to my bunker watching. There is a pancho over me and inside I am warm and tingly.

I am very happy. Under the pancho in my hands is a package of Oreo cookies. They are unopened. I got them today when the chopper came with the mail. I feel like hoarding myself and my treasure. I have seen dogs who got a bone and dragged it away to a quiet place to enjoy in private delight. Those dogs always had a very suspicious look and they gave it to anyone who came near them. I have this look now.

I am sitting in a quiet place and I am enjoying the anticipation of my treasure. I listen to the crinkle, crack of the cellophane and the sound is delicious.

Soon I will eat an entire package of Oreos. Next I will have the world's best cigarette. After this I will be vaguely ill and I will be ready to share the rest of my treasures from home with my comrades. I think this is what sharing is all about.

DANNY CARED ESPECIALLY

"I'm as tired as I used to be in the war protests. I'm just all drained." Said by an all-drained, very rich, shiny, pretty lady who owns her own company given to her by her own daddy. "God! I remember the gas and the vomiting and shitting in a ditch. It must have been July and no one really cared."

Wrong! We cared. We cared a lot. I remember turning to the Gunny and saying, "Gunny, stop the frigging war. Barbara Reap Mammouth-Smythe is vomiting and shitting in a ditch." So we stopped the war and we took off our helmets and we cared.

Jesus! Did we ever care. You were a legend to us Barb, a frigging legend. We even knew you said words like shit. We knew it was sweet from your lips. Danny especially cared.

I remember Danny saying, "I especially care." Too bad Danny got his legs blown off caring. However, in your honor, Danny vomited and shit all over himself.

BECAUSE WE LOVE THEM

The rain door has closed upon the earth. There are four of us cleaning weapons and meandering through time in the back of our thog.

There are beautiful smells in the back of our thog. Tobacco smoke is hidden in every corner. It weaves its way through onions, cordite, gun oil, diesel fuel and a dead musk smell of blood. When you come in you can root around to find just the right smell combination and pull it over you like a warm sweater.

Three of us are engaged within ourselves and our smells. Staff Sergeant Thieu, our interpreter, is watching us because he cannot find any comforting smells within our midst. We would give him some, but we don't know where his smells are hidden.

"You know why Americans here?" Said by Sergeant Thieu in the presence of alien smells.
"Because it is raining outside." Said by Corporal Crenna.
"No! No! Why you come Vietnam." Said by Sergeant Thieu and all the smells got up and left. We are very embarrassed for Sergeant Thieu. We are very embarrassed for America.

Staff Sergeant Thieu opens a huge smile which barely has room to spread out inside the thog. "I know. Vietnamese know." Thieu gives the impression of being part of a great and secret conspiracy of happiness. I can see the officer getting ready to give the secret handshake.

Then, like a clap of thunder in a pine box, Thieu explodes, "Because Americans love Vietnamese." Sergeant Thieu is immensely pleased with this revelation. The officer lets the bolt go home on his weapon and there is another clap of thunder.

"That's right. That's exactly, frigging right and I'll kill any son-of-a-bitch that says otherwise." Said the officer in much the same voice the bolt made when it went home. All of us are nodding our heads vigorously. Thieu has put on a Viking helmet and is singing old German army marching songs. The officer is dressed like Pontius Pilate and is washing his hands in Thieu's helmet. The Vienna Boy's Choir enters singing hosannas. God! I do love the little buggers.

THE HAMBURGER ELECTRIC

In country. I dreamed no nightingales on month one. Here the dreams were empty. Woke up three times to urinate. All is fear and watching.

Month two, the same with some ladies in garterbelts and hose. I thanked them and promised to return. They were so gentle with their eyes always open for the Hated-Cong. Woke up three times to urinate.

Month three and the ladies are rampant. Now their eyes are closed while I watch for the Hated-Cong. They have become too easy and I am suspicious. For whom or from whom do they close their eyes, and are they taking pictures of our military installations?

Month four and I am learning my evil trade. The ladies have become shadows holding dry clothes and hamburgers. Up two times to urinate.

Month five and all the ladies are gone. I lust for the hamburger electric and the atomic chocolate shake. Women are waitresses, vehicles of delivery. I am hungry and bored and I do not know where the war has gone. Up only once to urinate, but I remember where the war has gone.

GRANDFATHER

We are coming. Toward noise and chaos we are coming. There are dunes and marshes and sudden islands of jungle. The dunes are steep and the thogs pant, straining to pull their great carcasses over each obstacle.

Wait for us, sweet Jesus. We are coming to your aid. I am covered in sweat like an overcoat. The .50 calibre swings with every dune and gully, and it takes all my strength to hold her. Does she wish to leap ahead towards the battle? Go, my love, and I shall await your return with mead and cakes of honey.

No, I cannot send you off. They are all watching and I must complete what has been written. My grandfather is watching too. I am unafraid, grandfather.

I cannot tell him the truth for his me within his mind might die and his me is all I wish to be. And if this broke and fell, I would have nothing else left to be. I am unafraid, grandfather. See how high my head is held unflinching toward the fray? I can see the tracers now spilling out from a little place of battle to wander overhead. Where will they go, grandfather?

THE ROBE

He is hanging from a tree just outside our perimeter. The day is wet-hot and he is unconcerned. Many flies have come to him as supplicants to a king. His right arm is missing at the shoulder and he is smoking a Marlboro cigarette.

Jesus! You talk about your macho images. The ad executives are going wild. The cameras are flashing. " Hold that smile. That's it, a male Gioconda type. Fan-frigging-tastic! Camels and Luckys are left in the dust."

Walk a mile. Shit! Here is a guy so bad he's dead and still got one lit. That's a Marlboro, baby. Damn, there's a frigging ciga-rette. Want to know what they are smoking in hell?

Then, like a flash of light, the officer comes out of the ground where the big bitch with the spear and the loud voice lives. Little Willie's camera is sailing across the rice paddy like a goosed bird. "Don't mess with my man Albert. He don't smoke, he don't drink, he don't cuss and he don't mess around with women. This man has been like a brother to me. We grew up in Bayonne, New Jersey and . . ."

"Sir," said by Little Willie interrupting Mr. Stone in his third grade class at Vollentine Elementary, "That's the slope you wasted this morning in the spider hole." For a moment the officer's eyes look far away, then his face tightens like a giant gripping a tomato. "Willie, you are an unmitigated shit, you enlisted toad. Is there anyone here who can deny Willie is enlisted?"

Everyone quickly agrees that Willie is an enlisted toad. Six enraged men have become one. Jesus! Can you ever recognize the real thing when it drops in on you? The officer leans over and places his head next to the slope, then nods his head.

"That's the kind of guy Albert is, Willie. Did you hear that? Albert just said you might not be enlisted. I could tell you stories about Albert. He is quite a dude. Albert's real tired now though, and he wants to sleep in one of our nice green bags. So, Willie, you cut my man Albert down and very gently, as gentle as the wind under a gnat's wing. You put him to sleep and stay with him tonight because he gets lonely, Willie. And Willie, whoever took his robe—I pity his frigging ass."

THEY

They know about me killing the old woman. She stood up in the elephant grass and died. Three .50 caliber slugs, and nothing left to fix. Dead. Very dead.

They are watching me. I know because I am the Klaxton of Cromcrulock and two steps ahead of their simple minds.

God's wrath in a silver chalice.
Wind-touched feathers of a dead bird.

They do not speak, they only watch. I hear their voices still. She was Judas in black pajamas. She has killed me as surely as I have killed her.

They studiously avoid words. I am taboo until the new moon falls. Quietly, one drop at a time, the taboo will be emptied. Quietly, one drop at a time, we will all be emptied.

ZELDA WAITING

We are pulling out of Doc Lo today. The inhabitants are confused. There is much chattering and running about. We too are confused. We too are chattering and running about.

The whole damn American war effort is leaving today. Why are we leaving? Why did we come in the first place? Sergeant Brine says the press and politicians have sapped the public's will to resist.

I know no one is really responsible. No man, or group of men, have caused this madness. It is the Process. The Process itself is all consuming. It consists of massive bumbles, veins of pure ignorance, adumbrations of chaos, the joys of procrastination, a maddening desire to let well enough alone and to be forever alone with well enough. "Not another one, they are deadly."

We are packed in the back of a truck with all our paraphernalia and our travel brochures. A Vietnamese woman with a child in hand is framed in the center of the road watching our departure. She is standing in a gently rising sun, living in a postcard I bought for Zelda from Chicago.

Zelda was ugly eighteen when I met her drunk-speaking in a bar in Memphis, Tennessee. The spirit was upon me and all women were beautiful. I was an actor in a dream, in the midst of making one of the great movies of all time.

Every word I uttered was a charming. Soon a heap of charmings had piled up around Zelda until she was completely buried in charmings. I reached down and wrapped her in my silk handkerchief and took her home.

In the morning I realized Zelda was a ninety year old dwarf with a wooden leg. She also babbled a lot. She purred too. Sometimes she broke my heart, she purred so sweet. She purred doing the dishes, cleaning floors, and cooking dinner.

At first the devotion and the newness were enough. Then one day the sun died in my closet and I took myself away. I hid when I did it so I couldn't see Zelda or myself.

She came to the door waiting. I did not answer because I am weak for such things. When the gentle tapping stopped, I peeked out the window to see the passing. She was standing in the street where she will always live, sure of another tragedy and wondering why the beginnings.

Zelda and the Vietnamese with child are still waiting in my postcard. In all my recollections which I polish and rewind, still their shadows linger in the corners of my mind.

The Vietnam Conflict

Lies, Misconceptions and Half-Truths

Lies, Misconceptions and Half-Truths

American forces were defeated by North Vietnamese troops and Viet-Cong irregulars in the majority of battles in Vietnam.
Few statements could be further from the truth. The vast majority of engagements were won by American and South Vietnamese armed forces. The North Vietnamese admit to losing some 1,500,000 killed in action with another 300,000 missing in action. American forces soundly defeated the North Vietnamese and Viet-Cong on the battlefield, but failed in every important aspect of the propaganda war.

The CIA failed to understand the capabilities of North Vietnamese troops and Viet-Cong irregulars in their estimates prior to the Tet Offensive of 1968.
The CIA's estimate of these forces' capabilities was quite accurate. The CIA made no statements indicating the North Vietnamese government's military acumen in deciding to launch a major offensive. They did indicate that the North Vietnamese did not have the capability of successfully launching such an offensive, and they were most definitely correct. Anyone with a slingshot can launch an offensive; the CIA was assessing the potential for success, not the potential for making a military blunder of tremendous proportions. The Tet Offensive of 1968 was one of the most devastating defeats for any modern army in the 20th century.

Both American and North Vietnamese troops committed atrocities, and there is really no difference between the two combatants in relation to these aberrations of human behavior.
Both groups of combatants did commit atrocities. There is, however, an incredibly significant difference between the two governments in relationship to their policies concerning

such actions. The American government's policy was to insure that no noncombatants or prisoners were mistreated or harmed. In fact, the American government brought charges and court-martialed individuals involved in such incidents. The North Vietnamese government's policy was to execute noncombatants and prisoners when it served to further the government's interest in winning the war. Tens of thousands of noncombatants were executed on direct orders from the North Vietnamese government. Such policies were extremely effective in furthering their tactical and strategic goals. Village leaders and any noncombatants siding with the South Vietnamese government were targeted for execution by the Viet-Cong and North Vietnamese. The policy was quite effective in discouraging noncombatants from supporting the South Vietnamese government. The North Vietnamese have never denied this concept as they consider our concepts of holding noncombatants sacrosanct ludicrous.

The important point here is that for America the atrocities committed by our troops were aberrant behavior perpetrated by troops acting outside the directives of their government. For the North Vietnamese what we see as atrocities committed by their troops were for them governmentally sanctioned actions in keeping with winning the war and destroying the willingness of the people of South Vietnam to fight for a government that could not protect them against such acts.

The ratio of black Americans who served in Vietnam is far higher than their percentage of the American population.

While black Americans served with great distinction and valor in the war, there is no significant difference in the percentage serving in the war and the percentage in the American population. Eighty-six percent of those killed in action were white, 12.4 percent were black, and 1.6 percent were of other races. Ninety-eight blacks received the

Distinguished Service Cross and 20 received the Medal of Honor.

Bernard Fall died as a result of a conspiracy to insure that he did not write derogatory stories concerning American actions in the war.
This is absolutely without merit. Bernard Fall died when either he, or the Marine walking next to him, stepped on a landmine in a patty dike. I am certain of this because I was there within two minutes of the time the mine went off, to evacuate them to another location where medevac choppers could land. Mr. Fall and the Marine were both dead and lay within two feet of one another. If this scene had been staged by government conspirators, they were magicians. The area was in full view of some one hundred Marines and under heavy hostile fire from automatic weapons within seconds after the mine detonated. Mr. Fall, contrary to what appeared in some media, was greatly liked and admired by the Marines as he was one of us and actually stayed in harms way to get the stories he wrote. I personally saw Marines crying over the loss of someone who shared a common bond, and lived and died as one of us, no matter what his thoughts on the war, its reasons for being, or its final outcome. In fact, not one Marine I met even knew what Mr. Fall's thoughts were concerning the war; they only knew that he had served long in-country, and he knew more about the *Street without Joy* than any of us.

Agent Orange and other herbicides used in Vietnam have killed, or directly contributed to the deaths, of tens of thousands of Vietnam veterans.
There has not been one credible study showing any link between the herbicides used in Vietnam and illnesses in Vietnam veterans, not one. Vietnam veterans do not show disproportionate levels of illness in relation to other Americans of the same age groups who did not serve in Vietnam.

Vietnam veterans are unstable and account for a disproportionate number of arrests and psychiatric admissions in the American population.

This is blatantly false. Vietnam veterans actually show a slightly lower proportion of criminal arrests and psychiatric admissions than would be expected by their percentage of the population.

The South Vietnamese did not actually care who won the war and did not care about being free to choose their own government.

The South Vietnamese never were able to achieve true democracy, but this does not mean they did not wish to be free. Over two million South Vietnamese attempted to leave the country when the South fell to North Vietnamese troops. There is no way of knowing how many died trying to escape the incoming communist regime. They left in leaky freighters, and by every means they could, and many died in the attempt. Few actions could better illustrate how desperately these people wished to be free. We betrayed them by not bringing them into our country and into our hearts. We limited their immigration as if they had no special claim to our help and asylum.

South Vietnamese troops fought poorly and usually ran when under fire.

South Vietnamese troops fought bravely, and with great valor in the majority of instances. South Vietnamese troops did run on some occasions, but so did American troops. When you are poorly led, poorly trained, and poorly equipped you will have a tendency to run once in a while, but this does not mean that the majority of occasions in which great valor was demonstrated should be negated. South Vietnamese casualties were over 250,000 killed in action. In 1973 and 1974, after American troops had been withdrawn under the Paris Peace Accords, over 50,000 South Vietnamese troops were killed in action. This does not suggest that they avoided combat or usually ran under fire or had to have American troop support to be willing to fight. In these two years the South Vietnamese lost almost as many troops as America did during its entire involvement in the war.

The McNamara Line would have been effective if completed and was well accepted by American combat commanders as a deterrent for North Vietnamese incursions into South Vietnam.

There is no way to heap enough ridicule on the McNamara Line to do it justice. It was envisioned as a 1,000 meter wide area of cleared ground with landmines, motion detectors, barbed wire and watchtowers backed up by interlocking artillery fire bases. The Line started at the coast of South Vietnam below the DMZ and extended some 30 miles west and then shrank to less formidable barriers, as if it had become ashamed of its existence. Millions of dollars and thousands of Marines were wasted on this madness until it finally ended in 1968. Such a line would have been impossible to hold and defend without committing massive resources to a static defense of a tactically meaningless area. There were numerous other points of entry into South Vietnam open to the enemy. For such a concept to work, we would have had to close every major entry area into the country, and this would have been impossible even with all of America's resources.

Marine and Army commanders agreed on the strategic and tactical plan for the defense of South Vietnam.

This is untrue. There were great differences between Marine concepts and the Army's concepts of how to fight the war. The Army envisioned a search and destroy system in which mobile fighting units actively searched for communist troops, and committed the majority of combat units into seeking out the enemy no matter where they were to be found. The Marine strategy was to concentrate combat forces to protect civilian population centers, and to seek the enemy out when they threatened these population areas. The Army's concept rested on the idea that body count is the most important element to achieve victory—if we kill enough of them, they will give up and go home. The Marine concept rested on the idea that the most important element to achieve victory in a guerilla war is to maintain the population in safety and deny food, support and other resources to the enemy—if the population remains safe and committed to our side, then we will win. Obviously, the Marine units were under the supreme command of Army headquarters and followed the directives they were given, albeit with stated reservations.

The air war was largely ineffective in deciding the outcome of the conflict.

Yes and no. The ground support in South Vietnam conducted by all branches of the American and South Vietnamese air forces was superb, and many of us owe a never ending gratitude to these brave pilots and air crews. I cannot give enough thanks for the times that air power saved the day, and the sound of a helicopter overhead still makes my heart leap with joy. I believe that everyone who served would have the same praise. The contribution of air power to the major battles in South Vietnam is hard to overestimate.

The strategic campaign in North Vietnam was run by politicians and not by Air Force commanders. The ludicrous limitations imposed by the political pundits denied us the ability to destroy the enemy and his resources. There was no real strategic air power campaign. Air power was used as a bargaining threat for political goals and not as a major weapon for winning a war. It is amazing that Air Force personnel continued to fight the war under these limitations, knowing that many of the imposed guidelines insured that they would have a vastly increased likelihood of never returning, or getting a tour of duty in the Hanoi Hilton.

The Hmong were supported and fairly dealt with by America after our withdrawal from the conflict in 1973.
False. The Hmong fought bravely and continually against the communists, from 1961 to 1975. They formed a blocking and interdiction force against the Pathet Lao and the North Vietnamese during this period and were very effective. The Hmong were loyal and dedicated to the conflict. After 1975 they were relentlessly hunted by the new government and fled to Thailand and other countries. America owes them greatly and has never paid the debt.

The Montagnard people were supported and fairly dealt with by America after out withdrawal from the conflict in 1973.
Yes and no. The Montgnards are an indigenous people of the Vietnamese Central Highlands. Under French rule the Montgnards were promised a relatively autonomous state to be referred to as the Autonomous Republic of Cochinchina. The French gave them up in the Geneva Agreements and they became part of the Republic of Vietnam. Both sides used Montgnard troops during the war. They were excellent fighters and knew the area of the border around Laos and Cambodia. Both the South Vietnamese government and the North Vietnamese government feared an armed Montgnard presence, with good reason. After the North Vietnamese took over, the Montgnard continued the conflict at least until 1993. An uneasy peace exits between the present government and the remaining Montgnard till the present day.

At the conclusion of our involvement in the war we did little to help the Montgnard who had fought so bravely on our behalf. While official American governmental help was not given to the Montgnards, individual Americans were able to get small numbers of Montgnard who had fought with us to safety in America in 1988. Again, America failed to live up to its commitments to these brave people.

The news media lost the war for us in Vietnam and the majority of them were biased against American objectives in the war.

No. The news media were not loved by most combat troops after 1968 as the picture they, or their editors, presented of the war did not match the views of the average combat veteran. There were some media personnel who were highly respected by troops even when their views were at variance. This was usually due to the individual's willingness to actually be under fire to obtain information, rather than writing fiction while in a bar in Saigon.

I do not believe there was any conspiracy to present the war in any specific light by on-site news media. I do believe that there is what I call a "critical mass of belief" that colors our perceptions of the world around us. It works for individuals, professions, ethnic groups, religious groups and cultures. At some point in the examination of a problem, we develop what we believe to be a preponderance of evidence and then reach a conclusion. After that point, a critical mass of belief, we tend to see all new evidence in a manner that supports our already formed conclusion. It would be difficult to understand the news media's response to the Tet Offensive without such a construct. The Viet-Cong were effectively destroyed as a fighting force and America had an immense opportunity to settle the conflict if it had been able to exploit the advantage presented. Instead, America was bombarded with news reports indicating that we had been soundly defeated when exactly the opposite had occurred. This prevented the government from taking the necessary actions to win the war as officials believed that public opinion was turning against the conflict, and elections loomed in the future. The critical mass of belief in the U. S. had begun to turn against further involvement in the war.

When famous news reporters, who were truly admired and trusted by the American public, stated after the 1968 Tet Offensive that the war was lost, for all practical purposes they were correct; not because the battlefield belonged to the enemy, it did not, but because the future of America's commitment to the war was lost. It is commitment beyond all other variables that wins wars and our critical mass of belief had turned to the inevitability of defeat changing our government's commitment to a withdrawal with saving grace. Even North Vietnamese General Giap was astounded that our news reports had turned his massive defeat on the battlefield into a strategic victory.

The news media must fight for ratings like everyone else, and this has drastically changed our information dissemination systems. The truth does not necessarily sell if it is boring. Every day a new disaster, crisis, or scandal must be provided to pander to all of our desires for new and interesting stimuli.

It is also undoubtedly true that the strategic air war could have made an immense difference in crippling the enemy's ability to fight, but news reports of civilian casualties definitely affected the political decisions concerning limitations on bombing. The news media are in a battle for ratings and they must determine what will sell at any given time. When the little guy fighting the big guy becomes the selling point, the North Vietnamese have the edge, and this changes the slant of the majority of media productions.

This would not have been decisive, however, if politicians, who did have accurate information, had based their decisions on what they knew to be true rather than what they believed would get them reelected. Having professional politicians, rather than citizens who serve the public for a short period as an obligation to the country, makes cowards of us all.

The number of civilian casualties in Kosovo, Iraq, and Afghanistan received little coverage by the media, and politicians had no need to worry that this would be a critical point for the prosecution of these conflicts. Under these circumstances, the battle can be left to combat commanders who are making decisions on tactical and strategic military goals.

To say, however, that a media conspiracy existed during the Vietnam conflict, or that the media was to blame, is, in my opinion, false. There were not enough people with real knowledge of the conflict who stood up when the tide of public opinion began to turn, and said, "You are wrong and these are the reasons why you are wrong." I did not stand up and state this, and I am ashamed that I did not. I may have told someone that the information produced about the Tet Offensive was incorrect, or that I never saw any babies killed, but I did not stand up when it counted and try to build public knowledge concerning the reality of the conflict as I saw it. My voice would undoubtedly have made little impact, but it would have been in keeping with my own beliefs and it might have encouraged others, whose voices were more powerful than mine, to stand up and voice their opinions.

President Kennedy was in the process of getting America out of the Vietnam conflict when he was assassinated.

There is no credible evidence suggesting this is true. President Kennedy was rotating out some combat troops from Vietnam just prior to his death and this is the usual reason sited as confirmation of his desire to remove America from the war. Such rotations were not unusual at the time, however, and there was no call by military commanders for more troops until well after the President's death. President Kennedy had made no statements indicating his desire to withdraw American forces from the conflict, and there is no indication that he was not committed to continuing the conflict and winning.

It should also be remembered that one of the staunchest critics of our involvement in Vietnam was Vice-President Lyndon Johnson. His voice was silent during his period as Vice-President, but his ideas concerning the war were well known to President Kennedy and his key staff. President Johnson later did his best to carry out what he saw as the wishes of an assassinated president. President Johnson's views on the war are extremely well documented, however, and grassy knoll theories suggesting that President Kennedy was assassinated so the war would continue as ludicrous.

America lived up to its commitment to South Vietnam after withdrawing from the conflict in 1973.

This is absolutely untrue. America had committed to providing supplies and military hardware to South Vietnam and we did not do so. North Vietnam, however, continued to receive supplies and military hardware from China and Russia during this period. In fact, the amount of support for North Vietnam was actually increased by its allies. This placed South Vietnam in a position of having no long term supplies to replace losses on the battlefield, and led to the inevitable defeat of their armed forces.

We will never know how well the South Vietnamese could have defended themselves if they had the supplies and hardware necessary to continue the conflict. We will always know that we betrayed our commitment to them.

North Vietnam lived up to the Paris Peace Accords.

Not true. North Vietnam lived up to virtually none of its commitments under the Paris Peace Accords. By the end of the conflict, virtually all of North Vietnam's army was fighting in South Vietnam.

It is obvious that America's top officials knew that North Vietnam would never live up to its agreement. We basically left South Vietnam to die, knowing full well that we would no longer come to their aid under any circumstances, even with North Vietnam breaking every important aspect of the agreement. If this was to be the case, we should have stated the reality of our position, and allowed South Vietnam to make the best of the situation with the certain knowledge of what was to come. We should be ashamed, as a nation, for throwing our allies to the wolves and perpetrating a charade to cover our own unwillingness to fight.

All wars cannot be won in a year or two years or five years, and there are some wars worth fighting no matter how long it takes to get the job done. America is now paying a heavy price for our enemy's belief that we only fight in short installments when victory is assured with minimal casualties, and we will run if our nose is bloodied.

Semper Fi!